— SIÂN L

PROJECT
Kite

RED FOX

A Red Fox Book
Published by Random House Children's Books
20 Vauxhall Bridge Road, London SW1V 2SA

A division of Random House UK Ltd
London Melbourne Sydney Auckland
Johannesburg and agencies throughout the world

Text copyright © 1993 by Siân Lewis
Illustrations copyright © 1993 by Katie Ross
Cover illustration copyright © 1993 by Ken Brown

1 3 5 7 9 10 8 6 4 2

First published by Andersen Press Limited 1993

Red Fox edition 1996

Printed and bound in Great Britain by
Cox & Wyman Ltd, Reading, Berkshire

RANDOM HOUSE UK Limited Reg. No. 954009

Papers used by Random House UK Limited
are natural, recyclable products made from wood grown in
sustainable forests. The manufacturing processes conform to
the environmental regulations of the country of origin

ISBN 0 09 946151 X

PROJECT: KITE

I'm Gary Lloyd.
This is my family tree:

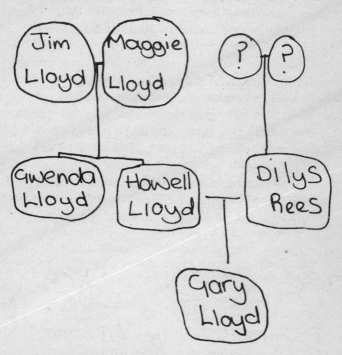

That's how I drew it last year when I was ten and in
Mr Griffiths's class in Glaslyn School.

Mr Griffiths was a new teacher then. He wanted us
to do a project on our village.

'How many of you have all four grandparents

5

living in Glaslyn?' he asked and I was the only one who put my hand up.

'Right then, Gary,' he said. 'You can do a project on your family. Make a family tree and ask your mam and dad to help you write in the names of all your grandparents, uncles, aunts and cousins.'

He gave me a blank sheet of paper. I took it home and filled up Dad's side straight off. I was going to write in Nan and Dad-cu Rees's names on Mam's side, till I remembered. Mam's adopted.

Mam said later that the two circles with question marks where her mam and dad's names should be had stared at her like eyes. That's what made her start looking for her parents.

So I left the family tree to Mam and I went on to do another project on kites. Thing is, the kites and my family tree got a little bit mixed up – like this.

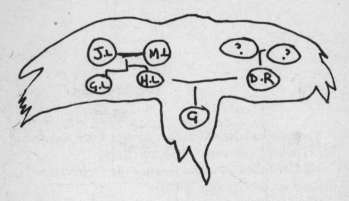

Family tree changed into kite!

6

KITES

First of all I'd better explain what kites are. They're not bits of coloured canvas that float in the air on lengths of string! The kites I'm going to talk about are beautiful birds of prey with red-brown feathers and forked tails.

If you lived in London, York, Edinburgh, Birmingham or wherever three hundred years ago, you might well have seen a kite hovering over your back garden. But you won't any more. Farmers and gamekeepers killed most of them. Now there are only a few kites left in Britain and they live in mid-Wales near my home.

Here's a plan of my village. I'm calling it Glaslyn

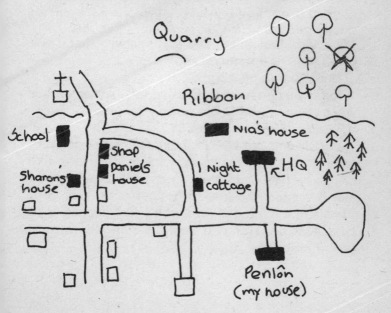

village. I can't give you its real name – I'll tell you why later on.

Glaslyn is just a few scattered houses squashed between the hills at the far end of the Ribbon valley. The Ribbon trickles out of the ground in the old oak and beech wood that froths down the hill above our village. Beside this wood the Forestry Commission has planted rows and rows of dark green pines.

My house is the one nearest to the woods. It's called Penlôn, which means *Lane's End*. It used to be a farmhouse, but we've sold all the fields except one. Dad works in an office in town. Mam used to work too. She was our school cook till last July. Since then she's been busy trying to trace her real mother.

MYSTERY BIRD!

Mam and I look alike. Our hair's so wiry that if you brush it up, it'll stand on end.

But Mam's a mystery!

Mam was brought to Glaslyn by a social worker when she was a baby just seven weeks old.

Where did she come from?

On the map our lane looks like the trunk of a very spindly tree and the roads leading to it look like branches. Dad and I were born in Glaslyn, so we're like two mice who live at the foot of the tree. But Mam's like a strange bird who's just happened to land near us. Her real home is somewhere on a far-off branch.

I drew that before I knew Mam's real mother's name was Eileen Mary PERROTT – almost a parrot! Mam wrote off to the Registrar General for her original birth certificate after she'd had a chat with the social worker. The birth certificate showed that her mother, Eileen Mary Perrott, used to live in Manchester which is a very far-off branch indeed.

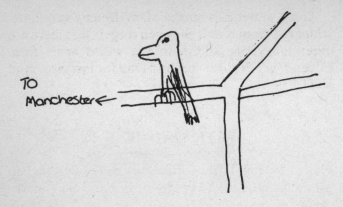

TO
Manchester ←

Mam went off to Manchester to look for Eileen Mary Perrott, but no one had ever heard of her. Even her house had disappeared. Then Mam went to St. Catherine's House in London. In St. Catherine's House they keep the names of everyone who's been born, married or died in G.B.

Mam found her mother's name there. She'd married again. Eileen Mary Perrott is now Eileen Mary Brown. She married someone called Arthur Edward Brown in Liverpool in 1969. That's all we know.

Finding a Perrott is bad enough but finding the right Brown is impossible. There are millions of them! But now that Mam has started looking for her mother, she won't give up. She's decided to work through the Perrotts in the phone directories to see if she can find a relative of Eileen Mary's. It's costing us a bomb in phone calls and letters.

10

And it sometimes makes Mam dreamy and short-tempered. Sometimes she even forgets that there are other interesting things in *the* world apart from Eileen Mary Perrott – me and Dad for instance. And KITES!

KITE MADNESS

Mam, Dad and I quite often look out of our kitchen window and say: 'There's a kite at the quarry again.'

The quarry is a hole in the hill opposite our house (see map). A long time ago people in our village used to get stones from the quarry to build their barns and houses. Now they just dump rubbish there.

Kites are very keen on rubbish. They hunt in it for bits of food. That's why they hung around houses years ago and that's why they come to the quarry now.

I've seen kites at the quarry ever since I can remember. I never even bothered to think about them much till two months ago.

Two months ago Jeff Jones came to our school.

JEFF

Jeff Jones is the man from the RSPB (Royal Society for the Protection of Birds).

11

He's obsessed with birds. He knows everything about them.

Jeff is tall and skinny. He hunches his shoulders and normally mumbles in a soft, shy voice. When Mr Griffiths was telling us what a fantastic bird expert he was, Jeff looked as if he hated the sound of his own name. His chin sank into the collar of his jumper and we all thought he looked a wally.

But – as soon as Jeff started talking about birds, he exploded like a Roman candle. He was ace! After listening to him, we all wanted to rush out and devote our lives to red kites.

'Your wish is my command, Oh great red Kite!'

Kites are Jeff's big thing. His greatest wish is to save the red kite from extinction, so that in a thousand years – even a million years' time – there'll still be the shadow of a kite hovering over Glaslyn.

See these two shadows? Which one is the kite?

It's the one on the left. You can tell him by the V in his tail. The other one's a buzzard. There are plenty of them around here. Buzzards are big birds

12

too, but they're heavy old things compared to the kite. They're always sitting around spookily on posts watching for prey. You won't often catch a kite doing that. The kite prefers to be up in the air. That's where he belongs. He can hover on the wind, he can drift, he can soar, and when he wants to, he can fly really fast through the treetops.

They're beautiful, kites are. They're not red like telephone boxes. Their backs are the colour of shiny chestnuts with a pale grey head and bright yellow legs. I've got to tell you this, because you may never see one. There are only about eighty pairs of kites left in the country and, unless they're looked after, one day there could be none at all.

Farmers are still killing them accidentally. When they put down poison (which is illegal!) to kill the foxes and crows that attack their lambs, they end up killing red kites. Jeff showed us a picture of a dead red kite. Its wing span was nearly two metres. It looked huge. Jeff said it had died from eating poisoned meat.

13

Then Jeff showed us a picture of two kites' eggs. They'd both been stolen from their nest by an egg collector, who was fined only £1,000!

Egg collectors are extremely greedy and selfish people who steal birds' eggs and keep them in boxes, so they can boast about them to their other egg-collecting friends.

This is a kite's egg. It's dirty white with brown splodges. If you leave it alone, a beautiful kite will come out of it. A live flying kite is better than an egg in a box any day.

That's why I can't tell you the real name of our village. This project could fall into the wrong hands. An egg collector might read it and come rushing to our village to look for kites' eggs.

But, if you're an egg collector, let me tell you now: YOU WON'T GET PAST THE KITE GANG!

THE KITE GANG

Aha! You didn't know about the Kite Gang, did you?

When Jeff Jones was at our school, Nia – she's a girl who lives on the farm almost opposite my house – asked him if he'd show us a kite nest! Jeff said 'No', of course. All the nests are kept secret in case they're attacked by egg collectors. In the breeding season the RSPB people actually sit night and day in the cold and damp guarding the nests and the eggs.

Question: When is an egg not an egg?

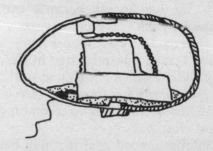

Answer: When it's a special device put into the nest by the RSPB to check how often the kites sit on their eggs!

'I wonder if there's a nest in Glaslyn that no one knows about,' said Nia at break-time. Nia and her friend Sharon had gone down to the bottom of the yard and were looking across at the woods. My friend Daniel and I had just got there before them.

15

Daniel looked round and gave Nia his special narrow-eyed secretive stare.

''Course there is,' he said.

'How d'you know?' said Sharon. She'd believe anything.

'He doesn't,' snapped Nia.

Daniel tapped his nose.

'You can tap your silly nose till it falls off,' said Nia, kicking her way up onto the wall and narrowly missing my face. 'I asked if there was a nest round here that no one knows about and you can't know about a nest that no one knows about, can you? So! Anyway' – she had to ask because Daniel's dad works in the Forestry – 'is there a nest?'

Daniel shrugged. Till Jeff Jones came along, the only wildlife Daniel was interested in was Sonic the Hedgehog. 'Well, we've got to find out,' said Nia, prodding Daniel with her foot, 'because if there is a nest in Glaslyn, we've got to do something about it. It's our nest after all.'

'Yes!' Sharon jumped as if the idea had actually stung her and she turned to look at Daniel and me.

Daniel and I didn't jump, but we'd both been stung too. Nia was right for once. It was *our* nest – that was the thing – our nest in our valley. We looked across at the misty green oaks which were just coming into leaf. If a kite had actually bothered to come to Glaslyn and nest in those trees, we couldn't just ignore it. It was our job to make sure it was safe.

That's when the four of us decided to call ourselves

'The Kite Gang'. We're the only four in Year Six in our school.

US

Nia

Daniel

in her own words: brilliant (Well, I thought of the Kite Gang, didn't I?), determined.

in his own words: ice-cool, razor-sharp reflexes.

Sharon

Me

in her own words: I can't think of anything to say. You say it.

We meet after school in the room at the top of Nia's barn which you can get to by climbing up the outside steps. In the room we've got an old black-board. On it Nia has pinned a photograph she took of the kite (a lot of sky with a black blob in the middle of it) and a calendar which we tick every time we see a kite. Sharon's drawn a picture of a kite in flight which is much better than Nia's photo. We've got bird books too.

We've been reading the books so we know what to look out for and I've been keeping a diary as well. I started it just after Jeff's visit. It was quite boring at first e.g.

March 14th: Saw kite hovering over the quarry.
March 19th: Saw kite swooping into quarry.

Sharon, Daniel, Nia and I went over to the quarry to try and see the kite at close range. It never came near when we were there. One day perhaps we'll try and build ourselves a hide.

In the meantime to keep ourselves busy we started making a list of all the birds in the valley. There were some birds which we heard but didn't see – wood-pecker, curlew and tawny owl, for instance – but we actually managed to spot and identify twenty-three different types, including the seagulls who fly in from the coast on stormy days. I like it when the crows fly to meet them and the two flocks weave in and out making black and white patterns in the sky.

Nia insists we saw a siskin, but Daniel and I both

18

think it was a greenfinch. That's just one of the birds we argued about. Lucky our kite's got a forked tail. You can't confuse our kite with any other bird at all.

March 29th: Saw kite over village.
April 7th: Saw two kites.

WOW! These two kites were swirling round and round in the air quite slowly without moving their wings.

Nia screeched, 'It says in the book that kites circle around like that before nesting.'

We ran out on the barn steps. The kites went on circling over the trees. From now on we'll have to keep them under observation every spare minute of the day. We want to see if they fly into our wood and if so, where. Once we've located the nest, we'll let Jeff know.

April 8-11th: No sign of kite.
April 12th: Saw a kite disappear into the woods, as marked on map.

This is it! The Easter holidays start tomorrow afternoon. On Saturday we'll be up in the woods.

April 13th

When I walked through our gate after school I should have known something was up, but I was too busy thinking of kites. For a start cooking smells were pouring like volcanic lava through our kitchen door. Mam is a brilliant cook, but she hadn't bothered much for ages.

Sid Radish was having one of his silly turns, springing in and out of the hedge and attacking my trainers.

Sid's my mega-cat (smoke-grey with a dazzling white ruff). He's called Radish because, when he was small, he dug up some of Mam's radishes and played marbles with them. Sid's big-headed. Normally he stalks around looking down his nose at you. You'd think he didn't care two hoots about anyone, but he does. Whenever Mam's been a bit low these last few months, Sid's always been around rubbing against her legs and purring.

It was because of Mam he was having his silly turn. Mam was rattling cutlery around in the kitchen and singing a song about a blue bird in a loud deep voice that was supposed to sound like Dad's.

'Has Pavarotti come to tea?' I yelled with my hands over my ears. (Pavarotti is Mam's favourite opera singer.)

Mam laughed. Her cheeks were pink and she was beaming all over her face.

'No,' she said. 'It's just a holiday treat.'

She meant the tea. She'd made blackberry pie with meringue on top and my favourite orange cake.

Even then I didn't suspect. It was when I was on my second helping of blackberry pie that Mam fetched the letter and set it down next to my plate. The postmark was Bristol.

'We could go down for a few days to Bristol,' she said. 'It's not ...'

'I can't!' I yelped.

'But it's not far and there's a zoo.'

'I've got things to do with Daniel and ...'

Mam sighed. She took the letter from the envelope and put it in my hand.

It was from someone called Bill Perrott. He said he was distantly related to Eileen Mary. He didn't know where she was now, but he'd try and find out.

'There's no point you going down there,' I protested. Mam was watching me. 'He's going to find out and let you know, isn't he?'

'Yes, but ...'

'Can I stay with Nan then?'

Mam had a strange look on her face. She gets upset if you don't jump for joy at the thought of finding the missing Eileen. But Dad and I have given up feeling excited ages ago. We just wish Mam wouldn't care about it so much. It's not life or death after all.

'Mam,' I said. 'I've got something I want to do with Daniel. It's important.'

Daniel, Sharon, Nia and I aren't telling anyone about the Kite Gang, but Mam guessed anyway. She looked out of the window.

'Something to do with your project?' she asked sharply.

'Yes,' I said.

'That's okay then,' she sighed. 'You can stay with Nan.'

April 14th

It's just as well I did.

For a start Nan was pleased to have me. Whenever anyone mentions Eileen Mary Perrott, Nan and Dad-cu Rees go quiet and watchful though they try not to and they never complain. Nan has even helped Mam write letters to dozens of Perrotts. I expect they're afraid that once E.M.P. is found, Mam won't think of them as her proper parents any more. But they needn't worry. Mam won't change, I know she won't – well, no more than she's changed already anyway.

Mam and Dad took me down to Nan's at eight o'clock in the morning. Sid was with us in the car, but of course he won't stay. He'll go stalking pigheadedly back to our house and I'll have to be chasing after him with bowls of food.

He's stupid. If he stayed with Nan she'd spoil him just like she spoils me. And Dad-cu too. Dad-cu'll probably want to take me up to town to buy me something, only I shan't be able to go. A real live kite on a nest is better than anything you can buy.

That's supposing we find one!

First I had to persuade Nan that I was capable of going up into the woods without being eaten by King

Picture of kite on nest drawn with fingers crossed (Note: Kites often decorate their nests with bits of cloth and polythene.)

Kong or a tree-climbing crocodile.

'I want you still in one piece when your mother gets back,' said Nan.

'Nan,' I said. 'You've always lived in Glaslyn. You've always played in the woods. You know the woods are safe.' (Not true as I found out later.)

'Okay,' Nan laughed. 'But you be back by tea.'

Daniel, Sharon, Nia and I met outside the village shop at half past twelve. Nan had given me money so I bought two bars of Kendal Mint Cake. On the Mint Cake wrapper it says: *Praised by members of many expeditions.*

'And by the Gang who found the kite,' said Nia as

she led the way along the path beside the Ribbon and crossed the field into her farmyard.

On her head Nia had a floppy blue bobble cap which she'd knitted herself. The bobble was only hanging on by one bit of wool and it wobbled like mad.

'Watch a kite doesn't sit on your head and try and hatch that thing,' said Daniel after he'd tried to tweak it off and failed.

'I wouldn't mind,' said Nia. 'You can take a picture of it, if it does.' She flung out her arm to make us all stop. Then she said, 'Wait for me!' and ran back to the house to fetch a camera – in case.

Sharon waited, Daniel and I didn't. We marched very quickly up the lane. As we passed our gatepost, a grey face popped into view and Sid Radish jumped out.

'Why didn't you stay at Nan's, Sid?' I asked.

Sid leapt up on the wall and looked down his nose at me. He was still watching us when we turned the corner.

From the field we heard a snuffling, scuttling noise, followed by bleating. It was the girls running through the sheep and lambs to try and beat us to the woods. Daniel and I both put on speed, especially Daniel who's got legs like elastic, but we couldn't get over the forestry gate fast enough and the girls caught up with us. We all tumbled over, giggling, puffing and snorting, then ... silence! We were in the woods. The pine trees stand in such dark silent rows that they make you go quiet and anyway we didn't want to scare the kites. We even held our breath. It was like being underwater.

On tiptoe we jogged up the hill to the clearing where the forestry road ends. It was filled with stacks of logs.

As soon as I touched the logs, out came my breath in a great gust. And out came a bar of Kendal Mint Cake. One nibble turned Daniel into a mountaineer. He went shinning up the logs and whistled.

I went up after him. He was lying flat on his stomach.

'Look!' he said.

Down below us someone had made a den by laying branches across from the bank to the log pile. It looked like Robinson Crusoe's shelter. Inside was a bit of sawn-off log to sit on.

Nia and Sharon scrambled up after us.

'Oh no!' cried Nia in disgust after she'd blown the bobble out of her eyes. 'Bet you James and Alun and the other Year Five boys have been playing here. We don't want them to see our kite. They'll tell everybody.'

Daniel and I slid down the logs and squeezed into the den. It was a really good den. We could see the sky in between the branches, but it only needed a sack over the top and it would have been quite dry. When the girls tried to push in after us, we stuck out our elbows and stopped them.

'We don't want to sit in your Wendy house anyway,' said Nia snootily. 'We'll go on without you.'

She jumped up on the bank and Sharon followed her, of course. As soon as Daniel and I went after them through the trees, they walked faster. Then we all ran quietly with our feet sinking into a cushion of pine needles.

In the valley it was a clear April day with a breeze blowing, but in the woods you wouldn't even have known the sun was out.

'There's a horrible pong of pine trees here,' said Sharon, pulling an anxious rabbity face at Daniel and me.

'Wow!' said Daniel. 'A-mazing! Pine trees that smell of pine. Must put a stop to that. Get me Mr Sheen quick. Sssss!' He sprayed and polished the nearest tree and flung a handful of pine needles at Sharon's back as she scuttled away.

Ahead of us pale slats of light hung down in curtains and the oaks sprawled to meet us with their feet buried in ferns and brambles.

'Sh!' said Sharon, stopping again with the sun on her face. 'What's that noise?'

It was only the Ribbon spitting its way along a cleft in the rock. Nia had already got to it and was peering into a little pool sheltered between the bank and a boulder. In the mud at the bottom, as still as a stone, sat a frog. I expect it was laying its eggs.

'Come on!' called Nia, before we'd had a proper look at it. 'There's an awful lot of trees over there.

We've got to get a move on.'

I stopped her with a wave of my Kendal Mint Cake.

'We're only eating half,' I said.

Nia stuffed her piece into her mouth as she crossed the Ribbon. You couldn't jump across because there was nowhere to land on the other side. Instead you had to step over and topple against the far bank. We pulled ourselves up with the help of some roots and branches and got plastered in mud.

'Yuk!' cried Sharon who was last up. The branch she was hanging on to swung up and clipped Daniel round the ear.

'Watch it!' he roared. 'You ...'

'Sh!'

Daniel hushed at once. Sharon had grabbed hold of him and was staring into the oakwoods.

'I thought I saw someone,' she whispered from the corner of her mouth.

The leaves rustled and showered us all with green and yellow sunlight. Nothing else moved. Nia rubbed her eyes. After a while she said to Sharon, 'It must have been the sun playing tricks.'

Sharon said nothing. She let go of Daniel and Daniel scowled and brushed his sleeve where she'd hung on to him. We'd all had a scary feeling. When Daniel spoke his voice was quite croaky. 'We'd better split up into two groups,' he said, 'and just check every tree till we find the nest.'

Sharon's neck disappeared into her shoulders. She

thought Daniel was just trying to get rid of her, which he was. She and Nia shuffled down a few steps, whilst Daniel and I moved higher up. We watched the girls move off, Nia first with Sharon hunched behind her, her wavy pale hair sticking to her forehead. Once they'd gone a little way, Daniel and I got going. We moved from tree to tree in a business-like way and peered up into the branches, but dust and bits of bud casing kept on falling into our eyes. It was no wonder we nearly tripped over the girls again.

'We're going round in circles,' sniffed Sharon blinking warily at us. 'I'm sure we've checked some of these trees twice.'

Nia broke off a twig and tried to scratch an X on the bark of the nearest tree to show it had been checked.

'Oh, come on,' I said and walked straight into a bramble that sent me sprawling into a mess of wet and gooey grass.

'You've lost your mint cake!' boomed Nia. I rescued the mint cake from the jaws of a tiny pale slug and slid it back into my pocket without giving her any. Serve her right for bothering about it and not about me.

'Let's go,' said Daniel.

We turned our backs on the girls. Daniel took the trees to the left and I took the ones to the right, but it wasn't easy because the oak trees don't grow in straight lines like the pines. We kept on having to zigzag up and down the hill. Things scuttled in the undergrowth, small birds fluttered and we frightened two moths that were exactly the same colour as a birch trunk. If we'd really found a kite sitting on a nest, we'd have given her a fit too. You get careless after a while. You forget to be quiet and you begin to think that you'll never find a kite anyway – that you were never meant to find a kite – so it doesn't matter how much noise you make.

I'd just swung round a tree and was giving Daniel the thumbs down, when I saw him stare at me with his mouth half open.

'Dan ...'

Behind me a twig cracked.

I spun round and Jeff Jones was standing there, his eyes sharp and keen as a bird's. He was holding a walkie-talkie at shoulder height and watching us as Sid Radish watches his prey.

'Jeff!'

He relaxed suddenly. The walkie-talkie swung down to his side.

'Hi!' he said softly. 'What are you two doing here?'

Neither of us answered. We both knew what he was doing in our woods.

'Out for a walk, are you?'

Daniel shook his head.

I took a breath and blurted out: 'We're looking for a kite's nest.'

Behind me I could hear the girls tiptoeing closer.

29

The noise stopped.

Jeff hadn't moved.

'We think there could be a kite nesting in the woods,' I said. 'We were going to check and let you know.'

'Jeff!' Suddenly Nia catapulted out from behind a tree. 'I thought you were an egg thief!' she gasped. 'I was just coming to rescue the boys.'

Cheek!

'Push off!' roared Daniel in disgust.

Jeff laughed.

Sharon came sidling up to us.

'I told you I saw someone in the woods,' she said happily.

But Nia was watching Jeff as keenly as he had watched me.

'You've found it, haven't you?' she said.

Jeff's eyes never flickered – but we knew.

Sharon's smile widened.

'Please can we see it?' Nia asked, humbly for once.

Jeff's eyes rested on each one of us in turn and in turn we all stopped breathing.

'Can you keep a secret?' he asked.

''Course we can!' burst out Nia. 'We're the Kite Gang and we spend all our time watching kites. But we haven't told anyone, not even our mums and dads.'

Jeff softened.

'Good,' he said. 'I'll take you once, but only once.

Understand? And you must be very, very quiet.'

'We won't come again,' I promised.

Jeff winked at me, then away he went, ducking through the trees. We followed like mice. The woods were magic, full of flittering sunlight and rippling breezes that sent waves of excitement washing all over us.

The enormous green mushroom of Jeff's tent bulged up from the undergrowth. Jeff stopped beside it. Ten metres away a rugged old oak had pushed itself clear of the other trees. It danced teasingly with the wind above our heads.

Then suddenly from the swaying branches came a gleam of steel sharp eyes. Jeff squeezed my arm. The branches swung apart and there she was – our kite – fierce and magnificent on her straggly wind-tossed nest.

The branches closed. No one spoke. No one moved. Nia never even took a photo. When the excitement became too much to bear, Jeff signalled to us. We slipped away through the woods, jumped the Ribbon, raced through the pine trees, charged down the hill – and *exploded*.

Mam phoned from Bristol at half past seven. I couldn't tell her about our find, but I think she may have guessed from the way my voice was vibrating. You can't sound normal when you've just seen a red kite on her nest!

April 15th

I spent the morning hopping around like a jack-in-the-box to stop the news bursting out of me. Mam and Dad arrived back from Bristol at half past two. They hadn't even had lunch, so Nan rushed to make them a fry-up.

Mam collapsed into the armchair in front of the fire, so I sneaked out to Dad who was standing on Nan's lawn gulping down great lungfuls of air. He hates being away from Glaslyn even for one night.

'Any luck?' I whispered from the corner of my mouth.

Dad blew out his cheeks.

'Not really,' he said. 'Bill Perrott wasn't expecting us, you see. We don't even know yet if the Eileen Mary Perrott he knows is actually your grandmother.'

'Yuk!' I said.

I never think of E.M.P. as my grandmother. I've got two grannies already.

Nan tapped on the window to call Dad for his lunch.

'What did this Bill Perrott look like?' I asked quickly.

Dad frowned. 'A little bit like Mr Evans the Shop, only thinner. I don't know. I can't really explain.' He went to rummage in the back of the car.

I studied myself in the wing mirror. I look like Mam and neither of us looks in the least bit like Mr

Evans the Shop.

'Here you are.' Dad was standing behind me. He dropped a box into my hands.

'Binoculars!' I couldn't believe it.

'Yes.'

'For me?'

'You're the only birdwatcher round here.' Dad grinned.

'Gary,' called Mam from the house. 'Has Dad given you your present yet?'

'Yes!' I rushed in and sat on the corner of her chair. The empty box fell to the floor and I trained my binoculars on the front window.

'What do you think?'

'Mega!'

Mam laughed and put her arm round me.

'Perhaps you'll be able to watch kites through them,' whispered Mam.

I'm sure I've got a brilliant red glow round me like the boy in the Ready Brek advert. The glow means: I'm a lucky person who's seen a red kite on her nest. Mam could feel it too, because she rested her cold cheek on my shoulder.

Through the binoculars I saw Daniel's huge face bulldoze up Nan's garden path. Daniel had the glow too. (Could have been from running!)

We went out the back to try out the binoculars and saw Merlin the Kite – that's what we call our kite now, because he's magic – slide out of the woods. It was hard to focus on him at first, but when I did, he sailed beautifully before my eyes like a ship past a porthole with the glitter of the sun on his feathers.

Daniel saw him too. He took a deep breath almost as though he wanted to suck Merlin to him through the air.

'I expect spotting the young kite will be our next great excitement,' he said.

But it wasn't.

April 17th

The radio woke me.

It was blasting out in the kitchen.

'Two men were taken into custody by police on Monday after two eggs disappeared from a kite's nest in mid-Wales ...'

It took a while to sink in.

We'd had a dull two days. I even went to town with Mam, because Dad said she needed a bit of cheering up. Mam spent all her time in the library looking up Perrotts in telephone directories. I wish she wouldn't.

Mam came up the stairs.

'Gary,' she began.

'Where was it?' I sat bolt upright.

'Oh, you heard,' she said. 'It didn't say exactly.'

I leapt out of bed. Puffs of mist we call 'gipsy fires' were drifting from the woods. Below me there was a screech of tyres. Nia and her bike landed with a clang on our yard.

'Stop her coming up here!' I yelled to Mam.

Mam only just got to the top of the stairs in time. Nia was already charging up. When she gets wild, she acts as if every house belongs to her.

'Gary's getting dressed,' said Mam.

'I've got to ...' puffed and squeaked Nia.

I've never got dressed so fast. When I flung my door open, Mam was standing squarely across the stairs grinning like mad with Nia fizzing up and down in front of her.

'Come on!' she exploded when she saw me.

Mam gave me a secret wink and dodged off downstairs. Nia belted along the landing like a torpedo, charged straight into my room and slammed the door so hard the draught blew my football across the floor.

'Emergency!' she gasped.

'It's not our nest, is it?'

'You know?' Nia shrieked.

'It is our nest!' My heart sank.

'No!' Nia's eyes were almost popping out of her head. I think she thought my brain had turned into a squidgy orange. 'It's not our nest that's been robbed, you fruitloop!' she said in a disgusted voice. 'Those eggs that were stolen, were taken last Tuesday. Anyway, what are you doing lying in bed when you know there are crooks around?' She jabbed me with a square finger. 'You come down to the HQ straight off. Now! I'm going to phone Sharon and Daniel to tell them to come too.' She screeched off down the stairs.

Mam raised her eyebrows at me.

'What was that about?' she asked.

'I've got to go down to her house,' I said, swinging my binoculars over my shoulder.

Mam put the bacon she was cooking for me into a sandwich without asking any more questions. Sid came for a share of it as soon as I'd stepped outside the door.

Daniel (crumpled and suspicious) and Sharon, (crumpled and worried) just beat me to the HQ. I could tell Sharon's pillow had lace on it, because there was a red pattern all the way down her right cheek.

'Get ready!' yelled Nia as soon as we stepped in through the door. She karate-kicked furiously across the room. 'It could be our nest next.'

'But our nest is safe,' grumbled Daniel. 'Isn't it? Jeff's guarding it.'

'*Nothing* is safe,' announced Nia sternly, pulling her jumper down. 'Nothing!'

A quick shiver ran down my back from the cold wall of the barn. It's the same shiver I get when the policeman comes to school to warn us not to trust strangers.

'We've been daft, you see,' gabbled Nia. 'We stopped watching the woods as soon as we found the kite's nest. It's now we should really be watching to

36

make sure no one gets to steal the eggs.'

Sharon looked at Daniel and me and in a flash we were all at the window. Nia whipped off her bobble hat and slashed all the cobwebs away.

'We'll watch from here,' she puffed. 'Our HQ's like a castle guarding the valley. No one can get past.'

'Well, they might,' said Sharon under her breath. She licked her finger and drew a sticky brown trail across the glass.

Nia got the message and charged off to get a bucket, some cloths and a bottle of Windowlene. We attacked the HQ window as though it were a bunch of crooks. We threw water in its face till it dripped down the walls. Nia jumped up and down on the outside with a sponge mop. When we'd dabbed it dry and given it a dose of Windowlene – magic! – there was so much sun coming in, we could have been in Spain.

'Loosenade!' gasped Nia. That's what she says when she's amazed. 'Loosenade' is what her great-gran calls Lucozade.

'Loosenade! There must have been a lot of muck on that window. I've never seen the sun through it before.'

She jammed the bobble cap back on her head. She'd forgotten it was covered in cobwebs till a ball of yucky grey floated down on her nose. The cap came off with a squeal.

The window was too dazzling. We could hardly look through it. But once we'd managed to screw up our eyes, whom did we see floating over the quarry? Merlin the Kite!

'We'll look after your nest,' called Nia to him. 'Don't you worry.'

I unhitched my binoculars and instantly Nia drew in her breath. But before she could say 'Gimme those', Daniel and I had slipped out together onto the barn steps.

Merlin the Kite obligingly floated up the valley towards us. By the time the girls came out, I had my binoculars fixed on him and we were looking into each other's eyes.

'It's as if he's coming to join us,' breathed Daniel, and he honestly looked as pleased as if he'd got to Level Eight of Crue Ball.

'Oh, hurry up!' begged Nia, squeezing past us. 'Hurry.' Her voice came out in a squeak and she gave my arm a sudden jog that sent Merlin zooming out of focus.

'Nia!' roared Daniel and I in the same breath.

But Nia was standing in front of us, pale-faced.

'Back!' she whispered. 'Back inside. Please!'

Please! If Nia says 'Please', something's up. Sharon, Daniel and I retreated.

'There's someone on the hill,' she croaked as soon as we were all inside the HQ. 'In that gully above the quarry where the dried-up stream used to be.'

We dropped to our knees in front of the window. Nia snatched the binoculars.

'Look!'

A shadow was moving up the gully. Daniel and I lay flat and watched it through the half-open door. It moved over the brow of the hill and disappeared.

'Someone's sneaked down the gully to spy on Merlin the Kite,' gulped Nia with a face as sharp and tense as Mrs Kite's. 'Must be!'

I don't know if she was right – you never know with Nia – but it was a horrible threatening feeling, a feeling that you couldn't trust the hills or the people around you. Up till then it had all been a game. When I ran home for lunch, I kept on looking over my shoulder. Even the sheep in the fields made me jump, because Mr Griffiths once read us a story about a king called Ulysses and how he and his men escaped from a giant by hanging onto the undersides of sheep. (Yuk!)

To make things worse there was a list of Perrott

phone numbers on our kitchen table with ticks and crosses beside each name. It looked like a list of enemy agents. I hit it out of the way and it floated onto the floor. Mam was juggling a hot plateful of sausages and chips on a teatowel. She pretended not to notice.

'Let's catch the bus up to town this afternoon,' she said, putting the plate down in front of me with a big smile. 'We'll have tea in a café and then come back with Dad in ...'

'I can't!'

'Oh, what's the matter with you?' Mam turned sharply and the teatowel caught me across the face.

'I've promised Nia ...'

'Why don't you promise me something for a change?' cried Mam. 'I'm your mam, aren't I?'

She was lobster-faced and puffing like bellows. She only ever gets like this when she's on Perrott business. It's rotten. It's like me when I'm doing my maths homework and I can't get a sum to work out.

'Is it about your project again?' she asked after she'd calmed down.

'Yes.' I swallowed a large lump of sausage. 'It's important, Mam. I won't be able to go to town hardly at all these holidays.'

I waited for her to erupt, but she just snorted in a reasonably friendly manner. She shook her head at me.

'You can go with Nan and Dad-cu,' I said.

'Can I really?' She laughed.

I glanced out of the window. I've got to stay and look after Glaslyn. Daniel, Nia, Sharon and I have drawn up a rota. Between us we're going to keep watch on the woods every minute from dawn to dusk each day. No one's going to steal our kite eggs.

I jumped up from the table straight after lunch. Mam stood in the doorway and watched me go.

'I'm not going for fun,' I called to her from the gate.

Afternoon

Fun – as if!

At first we felt like soldiers with our backs to the wall and not enough eyes in our heads. Every time a car slid along the road, I thought it was Attila the Hun and his hordes galloping in from the sea to

Attila the Hun, a vicious guy who flattened a lot of people in the Dark Ages

trample us. Every time a fly buzzed past I thought it was a Scud missile coming to get me.

Then nothing did come and we all got bored.

At half past three Daniel cracked. His stomach had been rumbling for ages and he was tapping out imaginary computer moves with his fingers which is always a bad sign.

'Let's go down to the shop to buy some Cup-a-Soups to warm us up,' he whispered desperately in my ear.

Nia must have been fed up too, because she let us go without any rude remarks. We raced each other across the field towards the Ribbon and Daniel's feet were actually in the water before he managed to stop. I crashed into him, fell back with a bump and Daniel fell on top of me.

We were giggling and rolling about on the gravel when suddenly we heard a noise from the other side of the stream. A tall skinny boy with a rucksack on his back was heading towards the quarry and grinning at us.

'Hello!' said Daniel.

'Hi!' said the boy. 'Does everyone paddle in their trainers round here?'

'Yeah,' said Daniel with a straight face. 'Saves cleaning them.'

He got up and pulled me up after him. By the time we'd brushed the gravel off ourselves the boy was halfway to the quarry.

I nudged Daniel. 'Egg thief?'

'No,' scoffed Daniel. 'Anyway,' he added, so I wouldn't think he was only thinking of his stomach, 'he'll never get past Nia, so it's quite safe for us to go down to the shop.'

'Yeah.' I wanted those Cup-a-Soups just as much as Daniel did, so we belted on down to the village.

Mrs Evans the Shop was sitting on her windowsill in the sun.

'Summer's coming, boys,' she called. 'There are visitors in One Night Cottage and I've just seen the first camper in Glaslyn.'

'Who?' panted Daniel.

'I don't know who's at the cottage,' said Mrs Evans in a sniffy voice which meant the visitors hadn't patronised her shop. 'But you must have passed the camper just now. He's Edward from London. He arrived on the cake lorry and he's just bought a pork pie for his tea.'

On our way back we saw that Edward's tent had sprouted on the river bank beside the old quarry and my binoculars were flashing busily at the HQ window.

'Unidentified object down by the river,' breathed Nia as the door closed behind us.

'That's Edward,' said Daniel. 'He's a camper from London.'

'How do you know?' Nia put down the binoculars and glared.

'Aha!' I tapped my nose. 'I'll tell you something else. He's having pork pie for tea.'

'A pork pie!' Sharon was coming up the steps behind us with a flask of hot water from Nia's kitchen. She sighed jealously.

That was the signal to break out the Cup-a-Soups. Nia drank hers at the window.

'Just because he's a camper doesn't mean he's not an egg thief,' she said. 'We've got to watch him.'

April 18th

Easier said than done!

By this morning Edward's tent had disappeared.

My alarm went off at *half past six*! At seven Mam came in with a cardigan over her nightie.

'What are you doing out of bed?' she gasped.

'Birdwatching.' The Kite Gang doesn't do things by halves. If we say we're going to keep watch from dawn to dusk, that's exactly what we do. Mine was the first shift.

Mam laughed and it was quite funny.

It was pelting with rain outside. I couldn't see across the valley for mist. The sun hadn't even bothered to get up on such a miserable day. Any egg thief that goes out in weather like this is stark raving mad.

Or clever! I took a peep through my binoculars and all I saw was a gigantic raindrop. I couldn't see Edward's tent.

Couldn't see the sheep on the hills either. Maybe

they'd all dived down rabbit holes to keep dry.

Just when I thought I was freezing to death, Mam brought me a mug of hot chocolate. She came and drank chocolate with me.

'What are you doing up then?' I asked.

'Can't sleep.' She pulled the duvet off my bed and wrapped it round herself.

'You should get a job,' I said, 'then you'd be snoring your head off like Dad.'

Mam laughed. Dad's snores were even drowning the raindrops.

'Perhaps I will,' she said as she dipped her nose into the mug.

She looked like a little old lady with the duvet round her. I knew what was keeping her awake – the Perrott business.

'You couldn't get nicer parents than Nan and Dad-cu Rees,' I said more angrily than I'd intended. 'I don't know why you're bothering.'

'It isn't that.' Mam took a quick breath. 'It's just wanting to know. There must be things you want to know.' She peeped at me over her mug.

I thought about the kite's nest. At one time I thought I'd collapse into a heap of dust if I didn't find out about it.

'Yes,' I said.

'You see,' said Mam, 'you're the only blood relation I've got. Your dad, now, he's related to half of Glaslyn. And so are you.'

'Yeah.' I've got enough second cousins to fill a

rugby stadium. I suppose for Mam it's different. Maybe she feels as small and unsafe as I'd been feeling the day before.

'All Dad's cousins know you just as well as they know Dad,' I said.

'I know,' said Mam. 'I know that. It's just that I'm nosy, I expect. I just want to know more.' She winked at me.

My cup of chocolate misted up the window. I tried to rub it clean, while enormous raindrops flew in my face and splodged against the glass.

The bed creaked across the landing.

'Come on,' said Mam, throwing the duvet aside. 'You'll never see anything through that window. Come downstairs and let's all have breakfast together.'

Dad shuffled into the kitchen ten minutes later and peered at me as if I were a Martian.

'Good grief!' he said. 'What are you doing up at this hour?'

'Birdwatching,' grinned Mam.

She opened the Rayburn door and let a burst of warm air into the kitchen. I sat opposite the window to keep watch on the hill. Nothing happened. Any egg thief who'd ventured out must have drowned long ago.

And someone nearly did drown!

Two people in fact.

The first was Sid Radish. He slunk into the

46

kitchen, wet as a fish, half his usual size, and collapsed in front of the Rayburn. By that time Dad had gone off to work, the rain had stopped and the fir tree by our gate was sparkling blue and yellow in the sun.

The sheep were moving again on the hill and the gully was full of white water. The Ribbon had lapped over its banks. I half expected to see Edward's tent bobbing away downstream.

At Nia's house something white waved from the window. It was Nia's turn to watch from eight to nine. From nine o'clock onwards . . . Brrr! I got Mam to give me money to buy provisions in the shop to keep the Kite Gang going throughout the day.

'Bring me some chicken portions as well,' she called.

'Coming, Sid?' I said, but Sid was fluffing up nicely by the fire. He just closed his eyes and gave me a silly look, so I went on my own.

I took the short cut down the lane past One Night Cottage. Years ago, if you built yourself a cottage in one night on common ground, you could keep it and all the land around it as far as an axe throw from the door. That's how One Night Cottage started off, but it isn't a little mud and straw cottage any more. It's been done up for holiday visitors and I could tell the visitors had come, because the tyre marks of their car had churned the lane into a swamp. I had to jump across the swamp on little islands of stone.

Mrs Evans was at the shop door. She waved, as

Man throwing axe from cottage door

I ran up past the churchyard, and shouted loud enough to launch the lifeboats on the coast ten miles away.

'Gary's coming!'

From the darkness behind her came a squelch and I had a shock to see Edward the camper dripping over the potato sacks in the shop. He must have nearly drowned. He was *soaking*!

'And this is Edward,' said Mrs Evans. 'Edward what?'

'Kipling,' muttered Edward. We were both staring so hard at him, his wet face was just about steaming with embarrassment.

'Kipling,' chuckled Mrs Evans. 'Like the cakes.

48

I've always wanted to meet Mr Kipling.' She nodded at me. 'Edward's been camping, if you please. Look at him.'

'I'm okay.' Edward shot me a spiky glance. Drops of water flew across the shop as he dragged his purse from his pocket.

'I'll soon dry off.'

'No you won't,' said Mrs Evans in a voice that sounded like a concrete block falling from a height. 'You'll never dry off. Not in April. The sun's not hot enough.'

Edward looked hot enough to combust spontaneously. He couldn't get his money out of his purse fast enough.

Out of the blue I said, 'D'you want to come home with me to have a bath and dry your clothes?'

Beside me Mrs Evans gave a satisfied sigh.

I'm sure she's telepathic.

I'm sure she put the words into my head. She even makes me buy things I don't want in the shop sometimes.

'Good idea,' she said. 'I'll phone your mam now to tell her you're on your way.'

Edward was opening and shutting his mouth like a fish. No one had warned him about Glaslynites. Once people fall into our clutches, they *never* escape. Our valley is a dead end after all.

'What do you want now then, Gary?' asked Mrs Evans and she rushed to get my goods, pushed them into my bag and came to the door to see us off, just to let Edward know there was no point in making a run for it.

Edward looked wild.

'Don't worry,' I said as soon as we'd turned the corner. 'Mam'll dry your clothes in no time.'

'That lady in the shop wouldn't let me get a word in,' gasped Edward, slinging his backpack over his shoulder. 'I only went in for a tin of soup and a box of matches.'

'Did you get them?' I asked.

'No!' He stopped in surprise.

I started giggling and in the end Edward did too. We stampeded through the mud pools, past the silent cottage where a flash of yellow paint gleamed like much-needed sunshine on the gatepost and raced down the road till we got to my house. Edward squelched to a halt.

'Is this your place?' he muttered.

'Yes.'

Mam was already out on the doorstep. Edward went pink as a beetroot.

'Come on,' I said. 'Mam's as bad as Mrs Evans the Shop. She won't let you get away.' I gave him a push up to the kitchen door.

Edward stood in the kitchen looking at Mam and me as if we were going to mug him. At the same time he was dripping pools of water onto the floor.

Sid Radish sat up, yawned, flicked his ears and considered coming over to give Edward a welcome.

When he saw the water, he thought better of it and collapsed on the chair again.

'Have you got any dry clothes?' Mam asked. 'If you haven't, I'll get some of my husband's.'

Edward spluttered like a wet firework.

'Edward doesn't really want to stay, Mam,' I said. 'Mrs Evans made him.'

A twinkle appeared in Mam's eye.

'Don't worry,' she said. 'It's no trouble. We're quite used to Bed and Breakfast visitors.'

We are too. I'd almost forgotten. It used to be fun keeping visitors and people who've stayed here send us Christmas cards every year. But Mam gave up keeping visitors last summer for the sake of E.M.Perrott. Our B+B sign is still standing, but it's covered by a blue fertilizer bag.

'I can't stay the night,' said Edward. 'Thanks, but ...'

'You won't have to pay,' I whispered.

'It isn't that.' He shook his head, as if it really hurt him to stay. He's daft, he is. If I were soaking wet, I'd want to get dry. I picked up Sid quickly and made him come over to say hello, which he did by hooking his claws in Edward's jeans and stretching.

Sid had another go at Edward's jeans when Mam was stuffing them into the washing machine.

'It'll take me ages to get these dry,' Mam whispered to me. 'And his sleeping bag's soaking. He'll have to stay the night, whether he likes

51

it or not.'

'Well, he won't like it,' I said. I was going to add that Edward looked more like a trapped rat than a visitor, when three sharp whistles made me jump.

Nia!

Mam was watching me from the corner of her eye.

'Mam!' I said in a panic. 'I was supposed to be down there by nine.'

'Go on then,' Mam said. She nudged me when she saw I wasn't moving. 'Go on. I'll cope with Edward. He looks as if he could do with a good sleep anyway.'

We listened. All was quiet in the spare room above the kitchen where Mam had made up a bed for Edward.

'Go on,' she said. 'I thought you had something important on.'

'Yes.' Merlin the Kite was skimming over the quarry with the sun on his wings. You can't forget about a kite just because there's a visitor in your house. Jeff Jones wouldn't. 'Are you sure, Mam?' I said, because usually I rally round and help with visitors.

''Course I am,' Mam replied.

I patted her shoulder and left the kitchen so fast that I didn't see Ron the postman's van, till it came skidding into the yard and nearly crushed my toes. Ron parked right in front of me, waved two letters from the open window, then when I got hold of them, refused to let go.

'There was a young fellow called Gary,
Who didn't know whom he should marry.
Then the postman came he-re
With a letter from Ni-a,
Saying, "Marry me, Gary. Don't tarry,"' he rattled
out in one breath.

'I've heard that one before,' I sighed. (This is
how Ron amuses himself in his van. He makes up
limericks about people.)

'It's your fault for having a name like Gary,'
grinned Ron. 'If your name rhymed with Arsenal or
Everton, I'd make up limericks about you playing
football, wouldn't I?'

'There must be a football team somewhere in the
world that ends in -ary,' I said.

'You find it then.' With a wink Ron let go of the
letters and swung the van around.

One of the letters was from Bristol. Mam still had
it in her hand, when another blast from Nia's whistle
sent me racing across the fields. The sheep fanned
away like ripples of water.

Nia was on top of the barn steps tapping her watch
and her foot and blocking the doorway.

'Where've you been?' she demanded. 'We are all
supposed to be here at nine.'

'I was watching at half past six this morning,' I said
in self-defence.

'So?'

Nia stepped back from the door and an amazing

gust of warm air bowled against my legs. Inside the HQ was a gas fire with Daniel and Sharon sitting on a rug in front of it. Beside them on the wooden floor there was a Monopoly board and three heaps of money.

'We're going to have a game,' explained Daniel giving me an elastic thumbs-up (i.e. your hand keeps on moving back towards your body as if it's on a length of elastic and you end up having several thumbs-ups for the price of one). 'And we're going to swap places. Each one of us is going to be on guard for half an hour at a time. Whoever's just finished being on duty takes over the place of the person who's on after. Get it?'

'Yeah!' Things were looking up. Even Nia must have realised yesterday was just too boring or she wouldn't have organised this. She was watching me through narrowed eyes.

'Where have you been to anyway?' she asked, as if she didn't know. She must have seen me and Edward from the HQ.

After I'd told them about our reluctant visitor, Nia sniffed.

'Well, keep an eye on him then,' she said.

'Yeah!' I said. 'He's sure to go off stealing eggs without any clothes on.'

Nia didn't even laugh.

Sometimes she's got no sense of humour.

When I got home for lunch, Edward's clothes were steaming on the Rayburn. Edward himself was in bed and the letter from Bristol was behind the jug on the windowsill.

3 pm

We drank a toast in Cup-a-Soups to Jeff Jones. He deserves a medal for sitting up in the woods hour after hour on his own.

Our room was so foggy with the heat and steam that I'd got tired of wiping the window and was keeping watch at the door instead. I'd just spotted our first swallow of the season darting over the Ribbon, when Nia got up to change places with me and brandished a wad of Monopoly money.

'Look at the fortune I've made for you!' she crowed.

'Huh!' snorted the rest of us. We'd all changed places so often that everyone had played each hand at least twice. We were getting sick of the sight of the Monopoly board.

Nia came and leaned on my shoulder, nearly knocking me down the steps.

'If I really were a millionairess,' she said, 'I'd use my money to build a special thief-proof fence around the kite's nest, so no one would ever be able to steal the eggs. And we wouldn't have to sit here all day.' Her voice was drowned by a jet screaming overhead. The sheep billowed like foam.

'Oh, come on, crooks!' sighed Nia. 'Hurry up so

we can catch yo-ou!' Her voice spiralled and she jerked away. A blob of red was moving among the rubbish heaps in the quarry. It was such a shock, I nearly choked.

'What's your dad doing over in the quarry?' gasped Nia.

(I'd better explain. Dad's got this bright red jumper that Nan Rees knitted for him. It's so bright, it's almost luminous. He usually only wears it on dark nights for fear of blinding someone.)

'He's disappeared!' hissed Nia. 'What's he doing? You haven't told him about Merlin the Kite, have you?'

'NO!'

The others were at the door by this time. Nia was trying to pull the binoculars from round my neck and almost strangling me.

'Oh, I know!' I gasped. 'It must be Edward. Mam was going to lend him some of Dad's clothes.'

'What's he doing over there then?' asked Nia in a hushed voice.

She dragged us back into the HQ and we peeped out through the half-open door.

Whatever Edward was doing, he wasn't hiding. In Dad's jumper he stood out like a beacon against the stones.

'Perhaps he lost something in the flood last night and he's looking for it,' I said.

Merlin the Kite chose that moment to come gliding

out of the woods. He comes out more and more often these days. Sometimes he flies right over Nia's yard and dips his wings to let us know everything's okay.

Today he must have sensed a stranger. There was a dead lamb in the field. I could see the crows picking at it, but instead of joining them, without a sound, without a movement of his wings, Merlin floated on towards the village. A flash of light followed him down the valley.

'Edward's got binoculars!' breathed Nia. 'Quick!'

She pulled my binoculars over my head so fast she nearly sliced my ears off, then she lay on her stomach on the barn steps and trained them on Edward. The rest of us didn't need binoculars. We could see quite well what Edward was doing. He was watching Merlin the Kite.

'I don't like it,' muttered Nia. 'What's he up to? Thank goodness your mam gave him that jumper so we could see him.'

I snorted. As if Mam had given Edward the red jumper just so that he could be seen by us!

'It's no laughing matter,' snapped Nia, elbowing me in the ribs. 'Binoculars mean birdwatchers. Why would he come to Glaslyn, except to look for kites?'

Why?

I don't usually ask our visitors why they came to Glaslyn. Usually they tell you. They go on about how beautifully quiet it is, how they've never seen the stars so clearly before, how funny the sheep are, poking their faces through the fence. Most of them wouldn't recognise a red kite if it perched on the end of their nose.

We watched Edward leave the quarry. He took a long time coming up the lane past One Night Cottage, but once we saw him heading down the road towards my house, the others pushed me out after him.

I crept up to my own back door like a spy. From inside the kitchen came a hiss and a rumble. The hiss came from a drop scone that Mam was cooking on top of the stove. The rumble was Sid's mega-purr. He was lying smugly in Dad's arms – I mean, Edward's! Apart from Dad's jumper Edward was wearing Dad's baggy jeans and his Wellingtons with the holes in the toes.

'What's the matter?' asked Mam, catching sight of me in the doorway.

'Nothing!' I squeaked. It had taken my breath away. How can you spy on someone who looks exactly like your dad?

Edward quivered when he saw my face. He quivered so violently that Sid dug his claws into his arm.

'Here,' said Mam with a twinkle in her eye. She buttered two warm scones and gave us one each. (Sid got his claw into a corner of Edward's, so Edward had to rip a bit off for him.)

'How about you two going for a little walk, while

I get the supper ready?'

I looked at Edward to see if he was agreeable, but Edward was already clumping at full speed out of the door. As soon as he got into the yard, he burst out in a huge explosive giggle that sent Sid leaping away in alarm.

'It was just your face,' he giggled. 'You looked as if you'd seen a ghost.'

'Not a ghost,' I replied with a grin. 'Just my dad. Dad hates that jumper, you know.'

That just set Edward off again. He looked quite different from the Edward of the morning, a bit mad, as if he'd opened up a floodgate that had been shut a long time. He stopped at last only when Sid jumped on the wall and gave him a good hard stare.

Across the fields I could see the shadows of the others in the HQ window. It was all right for them. They didn't know how hard it was to challenge a guy who's wearing your dad's jumper.

I was still trying to work out how to get round to it, when a forestry van purred out of the woods and filled in the silence. Nia calls forestry vans 'liquorice allsorts', though they don't look like sweets at all. They're the wrong colour. The yellow stripe comes in the middle instead of top and bottom.

No sooner had the forestry van gone past than I heard the growl of Dad's car coming down to meet it from the top road. I wanted to see his face when he turned in at the gate. It was well worth it too. Dad slammed his foot on the brake and juddered

'Liquorice Allsort'
(Doesn't look anything like a sweet!)

to a halt, pop-eyed, his cheeks like pink sherbet.

'This is Edward,' I explained quickly. 'He was camping in the rain and now he's staying the night with us.'

'Good grief!' cried Dad as he tumbled out. 'I thought I was looking at my own reflection.' He grinned at Mam who'd just appeared at the kitchen door. Then, 'Nice to see you, Edward,' he said. 'Borrow that jumper for as long as you like.' He patted Edward's shoulder as he ran up the steps into

60

the house. We could hear him and Mam laughing in the kitchen. It was the first time they'd laughed like that for ages.

That put us all in a good mood, including Edward. We've all missed the excitement of having visitors – and the special food. Mam had made a brilliant casserole with creamed vegetables, followed by crunchy apricot pie. In between mouthfuls Dad managed to treat Edward to all the history of Glaslyn from the year dot, with Mam adding details and dates.

Mam actually knows more about Glaslyn than Dad does, so it was odd when Edward said after supper when we were sitting on the garden wall waiting for Dad to reappear with OS maps and old photos of our house, 'Your mum's not from Glaslyn, is she?'

'Yes, she is,' I said. 'Well ... ' I told him about E.M.Perrott.

'I'd rather come from here than Manchester,' was Edward's reply.

Sid must have approved of that, because he walked straight over me and parked himself on Edward's knee, where he sat up straight and purred at Edward's chin.

'Hi-ya, big boy!' said Edward, giving him a sudden strangly bear-hug. Wow! Sid actually put up with it, and after the first shock, purred very loudly with his eyes half-closed.

While Edward was fussing over Sid, I watched

him. He had a pale thin face, the sort that Mam calls peaky and it crossed my mind that perhaps he came from a tiny crowded flat in London with damp walls and cockroaches and stuff. As soon as I thought of it, I knew it was a daft idea. Edward had a pair of really expensive trainers drying in the kitchen.

Just then he turned round and caught my eye.

'Have you got any brothers or sisters?' I asked.

'Two sisters,' he said gruffly.

The way he said it, it didn't sound as if having two sisters was much fun. I sometimes try and imagine what it would be like to have a brother or sister, but I can only really think of people I know. I wouldn't fancy sharing my home with Nia or Sharon, thank you very much, and I expect I get on better with Daniel as a friend than as a brother. Maybe Mam has got brothers and sisters somewhere. It's a funny thing. She talked about it once.

Dad came bustling out of the kitchen door with a handful of books and photos. When he was halfway down the steps, he suddenly raised his head, stopped in mid-stride and gazed across the valley.

Beside me Edward, who had been stroking Sid, stopped too. One moment Sid was purring, the next he wasn't. It was as if a Martian had got all three of them with a freeze gun. Even the air was shining. Then through the silence and the polished air I saw Merlin slide into view past Edward's head and float towards the woods. I saw him glide into the oak trees, just as if he were an arrow in slow motion deliberately pointing out his nest.

Suddenly I couldn't breathe. Dad was crossing the yard. He was handing Edward a book on the red kite and I couldn't stop him. A paw touched my leg. Sid stretched and swaggered over from Edward to me to make room. Edward took the book on his knee and framed it with his hands. He asked no questions. He didn't need to. From the way he looked I knew he knew all about the red kite.

'They're protected birds,' I blurted out. Sid looked up at me curiously. 'They're guarded. Even the SAS are guarding some of them.' That was a bit of information I'd picked up from the news after the recent robbery.

'I know,' said Edward, and he drew his hand over the picture of the kite just as if he were stroking it like he stroked Sid.

'I expect they're nesting round here,' Dad said and my neck cricked as loud as a bullet. 'There have been kites in our valley for as long as I can remember.'

'I'm glad I've seen one,' Edward said.

I looked down at the HQ. Nia, Sharon and Daniel were out on the steps. If only they'd heard. The way he spoke, Edward could easily have been a member of the Kite Gang. I'm sure he'd have convinced them as well.

'Aren't you lucky that cake lorry happened to drop you in Glaslyn?' Dad went on.

'Yeah!' Edward laughed.

Dad squeezed in between us on the wall.

'You're welcome to stay with us as long as you like,' he said hopefully. Dad wanted a change from E. M. Perrott. He wanted Edward to stay so Mam could forget her for a while, but Edward's face turned the colour of a ripe tomato.

'Thanks,' he said, shaking his head abruptly, 'but I can't. I've got to start for home tomorrow. My parents will be expecting me.'

As he spoke he looked at the house and I saw that Mam was in the doorway watching us.

'Ah well,' said Dad. 'Some other time.'

Dad opened an OS map and spread it out on his knee. Then he tried to get Edward to remember the name of the villages he'd come through, so he could show him the route on the map. Mam made eyes at me and I went into the house.

'What was that about?' she whispered.

'Dad just asked Edward if he wanted to stay on, but he's got to go home.'

'Oh.' Mam took another peep through the doorway. 'Nice boy,' she said.

'Yeah!' I said, but I was glad he was going. It was horrible having to watch him.

Once Dad had finished with his maps, Edward and I went for a walk up the road to the forestry clearing. We climbed up the log pile and I showed him the den. He showed me a stonechat's nest beneath the gorse bush at the forest gate.

April 19th

Something woke me in the night. First the darkness growled, then a sharper creak sent me rocketing out of bed and over to the icy window. A pale shadow was bobbing across our yard. Once I woke up properly, I saw it was the reflection of a torch from Edward's room.

The torch went out. I heard his bed creak and slid back under my own duvet. An owl hooted up in the woods and I thought of Jeff Jones in his tent, listening.

Next time I woke it was after nine and Mam was peering at me round the door.

'Okay?' she said.

'Yeah.'

'Will you call Edward before you come down?'

'Okay.'

I dressed in two ticks and went to knock on Edward's door. As soon as I heard his voice, I barged in and sent at least twenty fivers flying off the radiator into the air. Edward made a mad dive and caught one.

'Wow!' I said.

Edward had changed in the night. Back in his own grey jumper and jeans he looked like a drainpipe. Dad's clothes were hanging neatly on the back of the chair.

'You're not going to leave the red jumper, are

you?' I said.

Edward laughed and dangled a fiver over my nose.

'For you,' he said.

'Don't be daft!'

'Please.'

'No!' I dodged back out on the landing.

'Give it to your mum then,' begged Edward.

'No!' I said. 'Mam would go berserk if I took money.'

'Buy her chocolates or something.'

'She doesn't want anything.'

Edward grimaced and stuffed the notes in his jeans pockets just as the stairs creaked and Mam's face appeared between the banisters.

'Breakfast,' she said.

Sid came catapulting past her and started head-butting Edward through the door. He wanted us to start breakfast, so he could have a share of the bacon rind. Edward picked him up and I watched Sid's tail slap his back as I followed them down.

Mam was making a last ditch attempt to stop Edward going home. She'd made him mounds of breakfast, enough to anchor him to the floor. I don't know how he could eat so much and still stay so thin. Sid had his biggest breakfast since we last kept B&B visitors.

Through the window behind Edward's head I saw Nia on the barn steps. Bet she was dead jealous that I'd had time off from the HQ. Huh! She'd never have stood the strain of being a spy.

'Another piece of toast, Edward?' asked Mam's voice above me and I giggled at the look on Edward's face. The whole of him looked like a backpack full up to bursting.

'Watch you don't hitch-hike home through Henbont,' I said.

'Why?' said Edward.

'Because there's a weak bridge there.'

Mam didn't get it.

'It could collapse under his weight,' I said.

'Oh!'

Edward was laughing in a sheepish sort of way. For one nasty moment, I thought he was going to be sick. Instead he got to his feet and stretched.

'Oh,' he said. 'That was nice. D'you mind if I pop down the shop for a minute and then come back for my things?'

'Take as long as you like,' Mam said.

Edward winked at me as he lumbered out through the kitchen door.

From our back steps I watched his head bob along above the hedge top. A forestry van came past and shepherded him along the lane. Once he was out of sight, I had a pang of conscience and went to phone Nia, only Nia wasn't there. I heard Mrs Sanderson, Nia's mam, yell for her out on the yard.

'What about Daniel and Sharon?' I asked.

Mrs Sanderson yelled again.

No answer. Funny! Or not funny at all. Perhaps something had happened while I'd been fussing with Edward.

I raced up to my room and looked across the fields, but the Kite Gang was nowhere to be seen. Then I heard a noise. In Edward's room.

'Sid?'

I tiptoed along the landing. The door of Edward's room was open and there was Mam kneeling on the floor with Edward's wallet in her hand. She stuffed the wallet back into the rucksack in a hurry and fastened the straps.

'Just checking,' she muttered.

'Checking what?'

Mam got to her feet. Without looking at me, she shrugged.

'Checking what he's doing here.'

'He just happened to hitch-hike here on the cake lorry,' I said irritably. It was bad enough that I had to suspect Edward without Mam doing it too. 'You heard him.'

Mam shook her head. Quickly from Edward's rucksack she brought out a map. On it was the name of our village circled in blue and all the roads leading to it inked in. The ink had run when Edward got caught in the rain. Edward had lied to us. He'd always meant to come to Glaslyn.

Glaslyn. Even our valley can feel alien when clouds are scudding over it. The wind came sneaking in at the back door and ferreting round the house. It swept Ron the postman into our yard.

'Cheer up!' he called when he saw me looking grim at the kitchen door. 'What's the matter? You lovesick or something?'

Mam laughed. I felt sick all right, but it wasn't love. It was a different feeling altogether. I shook off the sound of Mam's laughter.

Ron looked slyly at me as he handed out the post. 'New rhyme,' he said. 'Gary – dromedary. Listen to this.

A handsome young fellow named Gary
Went to ride on a great dromedary.
One hump wouldn't do.
It had to be two.
One for Gary 'n one for Nia he wanted
                                    to marry.'

'I wouldn't want to marry her,' I growled. 'You've never had to put up with her.' But Ron was already skidding away.

The letters were just two boring bills.

'I didn't show you the letter I had yesterday, did I?' said Mam. She plucked it out from behind the jug and thrust it at me.

I didn't want to read it. The letter was from Bill Perrott and for one blissful night we'd had a rest from the Perrotts. All it said was that Eileen Mary Perrott had moved to the Elephant and Castle district of London about twenty years ago. No address. Nothing to get excited about, but Mam was excited. She was pink and puffing slightly.

I pushed the letter back behind the jug. Edward was creaking up the yard in his stiff trainers. I heard him slide something onto the kitchen table behind me.

'For you,' he said to Mam. 'Thanks for everything.'

'Oh, you shouldn't have,' Mam said in a sugary voice. I don't know how she could look him in the face. I couldn't.

Edward tapped me on the shoulder and gave me a big bar of Cadbury's which I dropped quickly on the table beside a box of Roses, in case my hands melted it.

'Cup of coffee?' I heard Mam say.

'No thanks,' said Edward. 'I've got to be going.'

'Will we see you round here again?'

Edward didn't answer. When I looked up, his face was a picture, as if different strings were tugging at it like Lilliputian strings on Gulliver's hair.

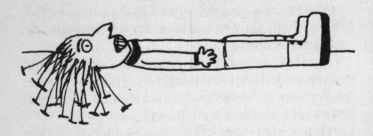

Gulliver and strings

'Well yes,' he said at last. 'Yes, I wouldn't mind.'

'Good.' Mam laughed, a deep contented laugh that bounced as if on springs across the kitchen and made Sid, who'd just come in, purr out loud.

Edward made his escape upstairs. We heard him pick up his rucksack. Mam was still smiling when he came down and shook hands with us and Sid. We all watched him disappear down the lane and went on watching till he'd turned up towards the crossroads. Then Mam put on the saucepan and made hot chocolate for the two of us and a saucer of flavoured milk for Sid.

Edward had left a silence behind him. All our B&B visitors leave a silence, but this was ghostly. Worse still, he had left a space like a vacuum-padded cushion between me and Mam who seemed so pleased with herself. I was glad when the phone rang and took her out of the kitchen.

'If it's Nia, tell her I'm on my way,' I called as I bolted towards the yard.

The wind was bulldozing its way down the valley. I fought with it till I reached Nia's lane, then slid down the sheltered tunnel towards the barn.

The HQ door was closed, the window empty, but I could hear Nia's voice inside. It stopped as soon as I went in and Daniel fell on his knees on the carpet with his back to me. Nia turned round.

'Hello, you!' she said in a friendlier tone than usual. 'What have you been doing then?'

'Seeing Edward off.'

Daniel blew loudly through his nose.

'He's gone then?' said Nia. 'Left Glaslyn?'

'Yes.'

'No, he hasn't!' Suddenly Nia was jumping at me and snapping her fingers in my face.

'He's been phoning down the village,' said Daniel in a sulky voice. 'And now he's hiding in the church-yard. Sharon's watching him from her window.'

'I told you there was something odd about him,' crowed Nia. 'You're useless, Gary! Bet you didn't know he was a crook, did you? Eh? Eh?'

'Shut up!' I yelled and I would have yelled more, if the telephone hadn't shrilled across the yard. Nia went off to answer it and that left Daniel and me alone.

As soon as she'd gone, Daniel swivelled round on his knees.

'I knew he was a crook too,' I said before he had a chance to say anything.

'Did you?' Daniel stopped looking sheepish and brightened.

'But I didn't know till this morning,' I said.

'Neither did we,' Daniel said eagerly. 'I wanted to phone you, but it's *her* phone.' He pulled a horrible face at the doorway through which Nia had disap-peared. 'When we saw Edward go off on his own this morning, Nia and I thought we'd better follow him because you weren't around. That was about an hour ago. He phoned from the kiosk, but we

72

couldn't hear what he was saying, then he went to the shop. Now Sharon's following him. She says he's hiding in the churchyard and keeping watch on the quarry road. He must be after the eggs. We think he's waiting for the shadow we saw in the gully the other day ...'

Daniel's mouth froze. Nia had just come running out of her house. She scrabbled up the steps. Her face came into view round the door, followed by the rest of her catapulting in like a beetle in a hurry.

'Sharon's lost him!' she panted. 'She thinks he could have gone to the quarry. Daniel, come with me and look for him. Gary, stay here.' Her pincer arm shot out, grabbed Daniel and dragged him out before he could protest. If it wasn't for Merlin, Daniel would never have let her do that to him.

He soon shook her off and beat her in a sprint across the yard. I slumped against the door, feeling like a tortoise dropped into a paddock full of racehorses. Ever since I'd found Mam rummaging through Edward's things, the world had slipped out of focus. All around me things were moving. Pale grey clouds chased each other across the sky. The young leaves slapped each other on the trees in the forestry woods. I even thought the stones in the quarry were sliding and the whole valley changing shape, till I realised it was Edward I could see, Edward in his grey jumper padding around the heaps of rubble.

I retreated into the shadow of the HQ so I

wouldn't have to look at him. Sharon was scuttling across the yard with her hands pulled up into the sleeves of her anorak. She looked more rabbity than ever.

'I lost him!' she said guiltily rubbing at her face with a sleeve.

'Nia and Daniel have got him. It's okay.'

I could see them both lurking in the hedge at the bottom of the field just across the Ribbon from Edward. Sharon rushed up the steps.

'Where? Oh!' She blew out her cheeks with relief and dropped down in the doorway, hugging herself. 'Was he really horrible, Gar?' she asked in a while, pressing her chin into her knees. 'He didn't look really horrible.'

'No.'

'What did he do then?'

'Nothing much,' I said through my teeth. 'He just lied to me, that's all.'

I shall never trust a visitor to our house again.

Even Mam had seen through him.

'Well, Gary?' she whispered when I dashed home at last for lunch. Edward hadn't moved from the quarry all morning. We'd all ended up watching him from the HQ.

'Well, what?' I said gruffly, looking round and finding her on the bench at the kitchen window.

'He hasn't left, has he?'

Mam had a gleam in her eye. I should have recognised it, but didn't.

'Do you think he could be anything at all to do with Eileen Mary Perrott?' she asked out of the blue, nearly knocking me sideways. 'It's funny that he should have come to Glaslyn on his own.'

So that was why Mam had been rummaging through the rucksack. She thought Edward was a Perrott. Sid appeared in the doorway and gave a wolfish howl. I wanted to howl too, only I didn't have enough breath to howl. We were all going mad.

'He can't be a Perrott!' I cried. 'His name's Kipling.'

'It isn't.'

'What do you mean?' Now I was gasping like a fish out of water.

'His name's Leggett,' said Mam. 'Edmund Leggett. It was on the bank card in his wallet.'

'But that's not Perrott!' I shrilled. 'Nor Brown!'

'I know.'

'Mam!' I shook her. 'It's not Perrott or Brown.'

'But he could be a nephew or a relative of some sort,' Mam said eagerly. 'Why else would he come to Glaslyn and pretend to be someone else?'

'Because he's an egg thief!' The words burst out before I could stop them. I leaned over Mam and squeezed her shoulder hard. 'There's a kite's nest in the woods,' I cried. 'I thought you'd guessed. You're not supposed to tell anyone. Edward knows it's there and he's after the eggs.'

'How do you know?' So much blood rushed to

75

Mam's face, I thought she was going to collapse.

'We've been watching him. Mam, you've got Perrotts on the brain. It's horrible when you go on about them all the time.'

'I know.' Mam's voice was quivering. 'I can't help it. He ... Edmund ... is in the quarry.'

'I know!'

The only sign of lunch was a saucepan dribbling potato mash on the stove. Its steam had misted up the windows. I rubbed a patch clean and saw Merlin the Kite slew round in the sky above the quarry. The wind tossed him in the air and drove him raggedly back towards the woods. Clouds of steam blotted him out, as Mam drained the potatoes in the sink.

The phone rang.

'Gary!' shrieked Nia, so loud it nearly burst my eardrums. 'He's tried to kill him!'

'Who?' I yelled almost as loud.

'Edward. He's nearly killed Merlin the Kite. Come quick.'

I rushed to the door and saw Nia and Sharon tear towards the Ribbon.

'Gary-y!' Mam's voice followed me down the fields.

Ahead of me sprays of water rose from the Ribbon as Nia and Sharon splashed through. Nia scrambled on top of the rubbish heap in the quarry.

'Edward!' she yelled, sliding down the other side. 'We saw you trying to kill that kite. Come out, you creep!'

Sharon turned round to babble at me. 'Edward threw a tin at Merlin. We saw him. He's trying to frighten him away from the nest.'

I leapt over the Ribbon, caught my foot on the bank and rolled on the grass. A pong of turpentine came sweeping over me, followed by Nia who trod on my leg.

'He's gone!' she puffed. 'He's done a runner, but his tent's behind those bushes over there.'

Even with a crushed leg I made sure I got to the tent first. It was empty. No sign of Edward or his kit. Mam was standing wind-blown in our back yard. An old disinfectant bottle lay wedged between the stones at my feet. I rooted it out and kicked it into the tent.

'He's not going to get away from here in a hurry!' I said through my teeth. 'Help me! Come on!'

Edward was rubbish. Nia and Sharon helped me fling stones and bottles and tins into his tent till it was messier than a kite's nest.

Messy kite's nest
(Kites' nests are rather messy. Honest!)

'He'll have a shock when he gets back,' panted Nia.

'I ... If he comes back,' quavered Sharon.

That made Nia and me stop in our tracks.

'Which way did Edward go?' I asked.

'I don't know!' Suddenly Nia was blushing like mad. 'I don't know!' she cried. You could tell she was kicking herself. She and Sharon were the ones left on guard after all. They'd had their lunch early. 'I didn't see him go, did I? What if he's got to the nest?' She began to panic. 'Perhaps throwing that tin was just a diversion. We've got to stop him.' She turned suddenly, skidded on a bottle and crashed into my leg a second time. 'We've got to stop that Edward Kipling,' she gasped pulling herself up via my jeans leg.

I shook my head.

Nia's red face appeared in front of my eyes.

'We've got to!' it said.

'I know,' I said hurriedly. 'That's not what I meant. His name's not Edward Kipling. It's Edmund Leggett.'

Nia stared at me. Her eyes nearly popped out of her head. Next moment, followed by Sharon, we were racing for the woods.

We'd have got there too if it hadn't been for Merlin the Kite and Daniel. We just felt this shadow over our heads and there was Merlin looking more ragged than ever, swaying in the sky.

Perhaps you've heard little birds squawk in terror when danger threatens their nest. Merlin didn't squawk. He just hung there like a storm-tossed sailor with his magnificent wings spread wide. At the same time we heard Daniel shout.

Nia skidded to a halt. Sharon and I bumped into her. Daniel was racing towards us looking so ultra-ratty that for a moment we thought his computer had broken.

'What are you doing?' he gasped. 'You idiots!'

·It only took a few seconds for Nia to blurt out what had happened. But all Daniel did was glance quickly at the woods and snap: 'Jeff's there. And we promised!'

'Oh!' Nia jerked like a puppet. 'But we've got to do something. What if he sneaks past Jeff?'

'We could phone the RSPB,' I burst out. 'They must be in touch with Jeff by radio. They could warn him.'

'Oh!' wailed Nia again, her face crumpling, but Daniel was backing me up.

'Yes,' he said. 'We could do that. And we could still keep watch.'

Above us Merlin had steadied in his flight. He seemed happier now that we were standing still. The trees were silent, hardly moving, their heads close together. We couldn't even tell where the nest was in its giant oak.

'If Edmund, Edward, whatever his name is, had got to the nest already, the mother kite would be

79

making a fuss, wouldn't she?' said Sharon breath-lessly.

'I suppose,' said Nia with a grudging shrug of her shoulders. 'Okay then. Let's phone.'

So we all began running back to the farm, leaving Merlin still on guard.

It was a mistake to let Nia do the phoning. She screeched like a berserk jet. No wonder the RSPB woman at the other end didn't understand.

When the message did get through, the RSPB woman sounded cool as a cucumber. She even laughed. She must have thought when she heard Nia screech, that every single bird in the world was going to be wiped out there and then. So she was quite relieved to find out that there was only one nest under threat, even if it was a kite's nest.

She sobered up after a bit and promised to get in touch with Jeff.

'I'll let you know what's happening,' she said.

Nia crouched by the phone like a guard dog.

'Shouldn't we be watching the woods?' whispered Sharon. Her voice was getting quieter and quieter. If we didn't sort out Edward soon, it would disappear completely.

'You and Daniel go,' snapped Nia. 'Gary can stay with me.'

Daniel rolled his eyes, but sloped off with Sharon. They were only halfway across the yard when the phone rang and Nia and I nearly hit the roof. Nia snatched up the receiver so quickly that it bounced out of her hands.

'Oh, Loosenade!' she wailed.

'Hello?' said the surprised voice at the other end.

'Hello?' gabbled Nia.

'Everything's okay,' said the RSPB woman cheerfully. 'We've contacted ...'

'But ...'

'We've contacted Jeff and everything's okay.'

'But you've got to do something!' pleaded Nia.

'Everything's fine.'

'But ...'

'Don't you worry. And don't you go up to the woods. There's no need to worry at all. Jeff's on the lookout.'

Nia couldn't even manage another 'but'. She just hunched shaking over the phone whilst the RSPB woman thanked her, then slammed down the receiver.

'Oh!' she spluttered. 'If that nest gets attacked, it's their fault. They're not doing anything. Nothing! They should have called for reinforcements. I don't think they believe Edmund, Edward, whoever he is, exists!' She slumped against the kitchen door.

Daniel and Sharon were looking warily in our direction from the barn steps.

'Everything,' spat Nia, 'is okay!'

'Okay?' Sharon couldn't believe it. She shrank farther into her anorak.

We all turned to the woods. The trees had knitted

81

themselves into a fluffy pale blanket that covered the hill. I wished I had X-ray eyes. I wished I could see Jeff and the nest.

'I wonder where Edmund is,' murmured Daniel. 'I didn't pass him on my way over here.'

'But we'd have seen him if he'd gone to the woods,' squeaked Sharon. 'Wouldn't we, Nia?'

No answer.

We all felt the silence. Nia wasn't even there. I looked over my shoulder and saw her appear in the kitchen doorway. She walked very precisely across the yard. No rushing. No jumping about.

We all expected some great announcement and it came.

'I've phoned the police,' she said.

'You what?' gasped Daniel.

'That Edward's pretending to be someone else, isn't he?' snapped Nia. 'He deserved it.'

She dropped beside us on the steps and let the silence play on our nerves. To think she'd actually phoned the police! Her mam and dad would be furious when they got back from town.

'They're going to send someone out here,' she said eventually in a calm voice.

Daniel swallowed noisily.

I shivered. I couldn't stop myself. I had a funny creepy feeling under my collar and when I turned in the direction of our house, I saw Mam. She was standing at the kitchen door and she wasn't moving.

Not one of us was moving. We were all too afraid we might capsize our valley.

Already our valley was growing. All this talk of crooks and strangers was pushing the sides apart. The four of us, perched on top of the steps outside the HQ, were getting smaller and smaller.

Us getting smaller

We felt the vibrations of the police car long before it turned down the lane. The squeal of the hand-brake shuddered through the stone steps. The two policemen who got out of the van didn't seem any bigger than we were.

'Are you the people who phoned about Edmund Leggett?' asked the driver in a flat voice.

'I am,' said Nia beside me, pressing her hands between her knees.

'Seen him since?'

'No.'

The policemen propped their elbows on the van

roof and watched the fields trickle away into the woods.

'You think he's up there?' the other policeman said nodding his head. 'In the trees?'

'Perhaps he's not there yet,' said Nia. 'But that's where he's heading for.'

'We'd best take a look round the village then,' the driver said. He signalled to his friend. The van creaked. Slowly it nosed round the yard and pulled away from us up the lane.

We could hear it edging, choking, reversing round the village, weaving a map of sound all around us. Nia squeezed herself tight.

'Bet you that Edmund is an internationally known crook,' she said fiercely. 'Those policemen knew his name.' Suddenly she exploded away from us across the yard. The rest of us leapt down after her.

'What d'you mean?' I yelled.

'I just had a feeling,' she cried, whirling round like a spider in a cup. 'I just had a feeling when I talked to them on the phone that they knew Edmund Leggett's name already. Sh!'

The noise of the police car had stopped.

'They've got him!' gulped Sharon wide-eyed.

Daniel leapt back onto the HQ steps.

'It's down by the shop!' he cried. 'Yeah! The police van's down by the shop! Let's go ...'

'No!' I grabbed his legs so hard he looked at me in surprise. I didn't want to see Edmund arrested. I didn't want to look at him again. 'We've got to keep watching the woods!' I reminded the others so they would stay with me.

Daniel didn't move. He didn't start heading for the police van, but he didn't stop watching it either. It was moving again. The sound gathered strength ...

'They're coming!' cried Daniel. He took a flying leap past me.

The lanes were growling as the police van edged carefully in between the spring hedges. Nia rushed up to the yard gate to meet it. The farm lane filled to bursting. A ray of sun flashed between the leaves as the van slid past Nia. It stopped on the yard with its engine still running.

We were all trying to stare past the policemen into the dark interior. A window opened and the policeman in the passenger seat looked out at us.

'Any sign?'

'No ...'

'Haven't you got him?' wailed Nia, tearing down the yard.

'Nuh!' The policeman sighed. 'Could have left the village, I suppose.'

'He hasn't!' cried Nia. 'He's going to go up to the woods. Perhaps he's there already!'

'Not to worry,' said the policeman.

Nia crashed against the van.

'You just keep your eyes open, there's good kids, and let us know the moment you see him. Okay?'

'But ...'

Nia was fizzing. The policeman took one look at her red face and began to wind up his window.

'Just phone up if you see him,' he said hastily as the window closed. 'No need to tackle him.'

The van was already swinging round. Before it had passed Nia properly, she was chasing it up the lane. She gave up halfway and turned to face us.

'They're useless!' she wailed. 'What are we supposed to do now?'

'We've just got to keep watch,' squeaked Sharon who'd gone running after her. 'He won't get into the woods if we keep watch.'

'You can keep watch,' snapped Nia. 'I'm going to find him!'

She shook herself free of Sharon and went marching off up the lane.

She was out of sight before the rest of us gathered our wits. Daniel was the first to shake himself.

'We can't let Nia go off on her own,' he said, curling his lip and looking at me from the corner of his eye. 'She'll do something totally stupid like trying to tackle Edmund. I suppose we'll have to go after her.'

'She's a blinking pain,' I said.

Sharon tried to come with us.

'You'd better stay here, Shar,' said Daniel. 'Someone's got to keep guard.'

Sharon retreated with her arms stiff like a scarecrow inside her anorak sleeves.

'We won't be long,' I said. 'We'll drag her back.'

'If we can get a dozen policemen and four tanks to help us,' muttered Daniel.

We both ran up the lane and when we got to the top gate Daniel threw back his head and roared, 'Nia! NIA!'

Of course she didn't answer. Instead we heard someone banging on a door. We raced up to the crossroads and took the lane that leads past One Night Cottage. We took it so fast that we forgot about the puddles in the tyre tracks outside the cottage gate. Daniel skidded right through them. A tidal wave of muddy water washed against my legs. When Nia came out of the gate, we both yelled in her face. It was her fault. Why was she so stupid?

'Sh!' hissed Nia so fiercely we both switched off at once. She pinched my arm. 'Can you smell something?'

'Oh, funny!' I snapped, brushing her and the stinking muddy water off my sleeve. Daniel was like a tomato and winding himself up for another attack.

'No!' she scoffed. 'Not the mud. Can't you smell something?' We sniffed. Nia turned my head towards One Night Cottage. 'Can't you SME-E-LL...?'

'Turpentine!'

'Yes! Not on me!' she snapped as I turned like a bloodhound towards her. 'I know it's on me as well, but it's round here too.'

'Yeah!' I'd caught a whiff of it.

Daniel came nearer. He hadn't been at the quarry

87

to smell the turps, but he'd smelled it on the rest of us.

'So?' he said.

'So Edmund's been here,' whispered Nia. 'He must have got the turps on his clothes in the quarry and we can smell it.'

Daniel and I peeped over the hedge. The windows of One Night Cottage stared back at us and we ducked down.

'There are holidaymakers staying at the cottage,' whispered Nia, 'but they're out, 'cause I've knocked on the door and I can't get an answer. So ...' She rolled her eyes in the direction of the wooden sliding door of the garage. 'He must be in there. When I count to three. One ...'

'Nia!' warned Daniel.

'ONE!' snarled Nia. 'Two. Three!' She charged through the gate towards the garage door. Daniel and I were daft enough to follow. I don't know what we meant to do – stop her, I think – but anyway we never had a chance. Nia grabbed at the door and pulled.

The door screeched. We just had time to look inside the garage – it was empty apart from a sprinkling of yellow paint and a SMELL – then a furious thumping from the direction of the cottage made our bones rattle. The top part of the bathroom window opened and an angry voice yelled through a cloud of steam: 'What do you kids think you're doing?'

'There's a dangerous criminal on the loose,' Nia

yelled back quick as a flash. 'Have you seen him? His name's Edmund Leggett. The police have told us to be on the lookout for him.'

Two startled eyes peeped through the gap and the voice said doubtfully, 'Well he's not here.'

'No,' said Nia. 'Well, let us know if you see him. He's tall and skinny. Dressed in grey.'

'Yeah. 'Course I will.' The man in the bathroom paused to wipe the steam from his eyes. By the time he looked out again, we'd gone. Daniel was hustling Nia out through the gate.

'You've scared that poor guy,' he hissed in her ear.

'Don't care. He deserved it,' said Nia with her nose in the air. 'Okay, so Edmund isn't there, but that smell was in his garage. So that man must have been chucking smelly old rubbish in our quarry. He should take it back with him to wherever he's come from and dump it there.'

Sharon was watching for us on the barn steps. We could see her, still scarecrow-like, with her back to the wall.

'Seen anything?' demanded Nia when we got down to the yard.

Sharon shook her head quickly. Her eyes were watering from so much watching. She dabbed them with her sleeves. The sky was pale and glassy and squeezing down on our heads.

'Well, something's got to happen,' said Nia. 'And soon.'

April 20th

The night growled again. I leapt out of bed, but the valley lay swathed in darkness, the sky just faintly tinged with grey.

A draught wormed its way round the window and a thoughtful meow came from the yard below, as Sid padded past in search of mice.

At half past six it was Mam who woke me, Mam in her dressing-gown crossing the yard. She saw me at the window and came upstairs, bringing with her a shiver of cold wind.

'Where have you been?' I asked.

'I couldn't sleep.'

We both watched the sun poke its fingers into the valley.

'You haven't seen Edmund?' I asked.

Mam shook her head.

'Where d'you think he is?'

'If you're right about him being an egg thief, he's in the woods, isn't he?' she said. But I could see she didn't believe it. She took hold of my hand and led me down to the kitchen for our morning cup of chocolate.

I opened the door to let the light in. Mam stood at my shoulder.

'Where would he sleep if he were in the woods?' she murmured. 'His tent's still in the quarry.'

The valley around us was shiny with dew. I almost expected to see Edmund's footprints imprinted darkly on the gleaming grass, leading from the river across to the woods. Instead I saw Sid Radish creep out from behind our log pile where he'd made himself a den.

My heart leapt. 'Mam!'

She flushed.

'The ... There's this den,' I said, 'this den we found and I showed it to him.'

Mam glanced across. It was dark in the woods, the trees as black as night. Anyone in the woods would still be sleeping. I stepped outside.

'Gary!' said Mam.

'It's okay,' I said without looking back. 'I'm just going up to check. I shan't be long.'

'Gary!' Mam's voice followed me down the yard. So did Sid. He streaked past me to the gate, waited with his ears flat, then streaked ahead again. He turned round at the entrance to the forestry land and watched me.

I wished I could move like him, silent as a shadow and fast, but my legs were tingling all over. I wished he'd come with me, but you can't make Sid do anything he doesn't want. With a condescending meow, his tail up in the air, he stalked past me and minced back home.

Meanie!

I filled my lungs and dived into the trees to get it over with quick. The sky slid like a conveyor belt overhead and dragged me wheezing on my jelly legs towards the clearing, where stacks of logs sent grey-blue shadows rolling towards me. Beside them flashed a sudden light.

It scared me so much I swung away, but it was only the sun. The sun had found the clearing before me. It was lapping the condensation off the roof of a forestry van and sliding down the windscreen. It was morning in the woods and I ran for the log piles.

'E ... Edmund!' I tried to make my voice sound gruff.

The den that Daniel had found was in shadow.

'Edmund?'

I rushed at it ... and it was empty. To make sure, I flattened myself against the log pile and let the sun creep past. It fastened on an unused match that lay like a red-eyed worm on the churned-up leaf mould at the entrance to the den. When I picked it up, it was so damp that the red stuff on the tip came off in my hand. I hoped Edmund had frozen.

'Gary!' Mam's voice reached me, very thin, through the trees.

I backed away. A faint familiar smell hung over the clearing. The forestry van clicked. I ran towards it, but it was empty apart from a heap of tyres. And it was wet.

'Gary.'

Mam was standing just inside the clearing.

'There's no one here, Mam,' I said. I'd wanted him to be there. I wanted to show him up in front of her and prove he wasn't a Perrott.

Mam nodded. She blew her hair back from her eyes.

'Then we can go back down again,' she said, pushing her hand through my arm and pulling me away.

Dad was waiting for us at the kitchen door with his head poking out like an inquisitive hen.

'What on earth's happening?' he called.

I let Mam explain to him. The phone was ringing and I knew quite well who was at the other end. I was right too. Nia's voice rushed in a torrent down the line.

'What's happening?' she demanded. 'Why are you and your mam rushing in and out of the woods like rabbits?'

'False alarm,' I said and sniffed.

Nia sniffed too, but she couldn't have smelled what I was smelling, a sickly mixture of paint and turps. I put the phone down and went back out to the kitchen.

Mam and Dad were still talking in the yard. Our house looked like the *Marie Celeste* with two full chocolate mugs skinning on the table. Sid knows he's not allowed on the table to drink it, but he was standing hopefully on guard.

Once Dad had gone, Mam and I stood guard at the kitchen window and watched the lane that goes past our house. If Edmund was still in Glaslyn, something was going to happen soon. Nia and Sharon watched the fields from the HQ. Daniel got out his fishing tackle and pretended to fish in the Ribbon just

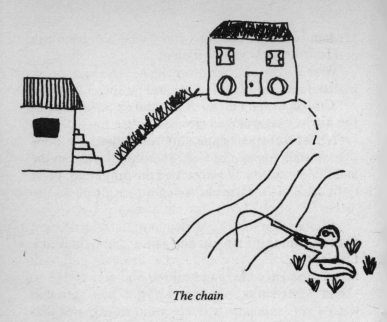

The chain

opposite Edmund's abandoned tent. We'd set up a chain across the valley. No one could get past us without being seen.

Above us the trees puffed out drifts of mist like the signals of attacking Indians, but Edmund didn't come. By ten o'clock Nia was on the phone.

'He can't be up in the woods or he'd have done something by now,' she said. 'He must be hiding somewhere in the village. Ha ha to him! I hope he tries to sneak past us and we get him.'

Mam came back into the house and picked up a chocolate biscuit from the kitchen table. She and I had almost finished a whole packet between us. I put my hand on her shoulder.

'Hope he's okay,' she sighed.

'Who?'

'Edmund.'

''Course he is!' I let go of her and slumped against the kitchen door. What was she bothering with him for? Edmund was all right. It was what he'd done that was all wrong. He'd made all the clocks in the valley slow down. We were all drowning in time.

'Want a biscuit?' asked Mam.

'No.' I stumped off down the yard.

Sharon went off to dinner first, then she took Daniel's place. She'd brought a drawing pad with her. I could see the pages blow. She was trying to sketch a heron that was pretending to be a statue in the water just downstream. Nia was sitting as still as the heron on the HQ steps.

Sid and I played in the yard. Mam switched on athletics on the telly, so we could hear the commentary and get excited about something far enough away.

By teatime Nia got so impatient, she phoned the RSPB.

'Everything's okay,' said the woman at the end of the line.

'How do you know?' demanded Nia. 'Perhaps the voice you can hear on the walkie-talkie isn't Jeff's.'

The RSPB woman chuckled. 'Everything is fine - really! If anything happens, we'll let you know.'

Nia ran over the field to tell me that.

'It's all right for her,' said Nia. 'She's not in Glaslyn.'

After she'd gone, Mam said, 'I think I'll phone too.'

'Phone who?' As if I didn't know! She'd been winding up to it all afternoon.

'Directory Inquiries. I'll ask for the numbers of any Leggetts in London.'

Her fingers touched my cheek and left a damp patch. Even when the sun had lapped it away, I could feel it there.

Yellow shadows kept dancing in front of my eyes and I searched for Edmund amongst them. It was like looking for an evil spirit. And it was worse when Mam came out with a jumble of telephone numbers. She'd done too much of that already.

'That's daft,' I snapped.

'This is how detectives work,' said Mam retreating to the house and leaving me on pins.

Nia was pacing up and down on the barn steps. From down by the stream Daniel raised his hand. I could feel the lines of energy passing between us like an electric fence. Edmund would never get past us in daylight ... unless he really was a spirit and could fly!

As the sun began edging towards the hill and the crows started flying home, Nia came jogging over the fields. She pushed through the hedge, put her hands on her hips and stared at me in an annoying way.

'Gary!' she said. 'Can you stay awake all night?'

96

Before I had time to do anything other than look amazed, she snapped, 'Well, someone's got to in case that creep tries to get past and your house is the only one on the lane. Pooh! I thought we'd have got him by now.' She glowered at me as if it was my fault. The glower went on a long time and ended in a loud sniff. 'You've got that stuff on you again,' she said.

'I know!' She was worse than Sid sniffing round my hands.

'Where's it from?'

'The forestry van in the woods.'

Nia raised her eyebrows. She flopped sideways against the gate. 'That forestry va ...'

Her voice just stopped.

When I looked up her mouth was open. A shrill metallic howl came out that seemed to last for ever. It set my teeth on edge. It smashed the air into fragments. It sent two birds tossing raggedly in the sky above the woods.

Two kites!

Mrs Kite had left her nest.

Nia had already started running towards the woods. Before I could follow, the lane behind us began to purr. A forestry van slewed round the corner from the direction of the village. It caught Nia by surprise and sent her diving headfirst into the hedge. The van stopped with a squeal of brakes.

'Are you okay?' called an anxious voice.

Nia disentangled herself from a bramble and took

one look at the driver's face.

'Jeff!' she wailed. 'Jeff Jones!'

Jeff was out of the van in a flash and kneeling beside her. The way she'd wailed he must have thought she'd broken every bone in her body.

'Are you all right?' he asked.

'Why have you left the nest?' cried Nia, throwing herself at him.

'Eh?' Jeff turned to me, but the look on my face must have startled him too.

'WHY HAVE YOU LEFT THE NEST?' yelled Nia. She grabbed hold of Jeff's shoulders.

'Well, I don't stay up there all the time,' Jeff said sharply.

'You don't?' That was me exploding. Jeff was caught between us.

'No, I don't,' he said. 'There's someone else guarding the nest. We take it in turns.'

Nia looked at me. How could anyone else be up in the woods? We'd been keeping watch all the time. It didn't make sense. I think for a moment we both thought Jeff was a crook.

'It's all right.' Carefully Jeff prised Nia's hands away from his collar. 'The nest is quite safe.'

'Safe!' wailed Nia. She pointed and it was then that Jeff saw the two kites whirling over the trees. His whole face stiffened as though someone had tightened a screw in his head.

'Something must have unsettled them,' he said at last in a breathy voice. 'They get unsettled easily, but

98

as long as the mother kite goes back to her nest, everything's okay. It's okay.'

'Check,' snapped Nia.

'Yeah.' Jeff shot back into his van. The van jerked away leaving a tremble behind it in the air.

Daniel and Sharon came thumping over the field. They scrambled over the hedge and nearly landed on top of a collapsed Nia.

'What's wrong?' cried Sharon.

'We've failed.' Nia lifted her head. There were two bright spots on her cheeks. 'We've failed!' she wailed. 'Jeff's been able to creep in and out of the woods without us seeing him. He's been using a forestry van. If he can get past us, anyone can. Edmund's probably up there now.'

'There's another forestry van up in the woods,' I said suddenly. 'And it's got tyres in it.'

'Tyres?' said Daniel. 'That's odd. What would a forestry van be doing with a load of tyres?'

The valley started growing again. The field stretched never-endingly beneath our feet. There was no time to go up into the woods to check on the forestry van. We just knew something had to be wrong so we did the only thing we could possibly do. We ran to the nest in the hope that we'd save it. As we ran, a shadow passed overhead. Merlin the Kite arrowed straight down the valley, slewed round and came back at top speed.

'Nia!' gasped Sharon.

99

Nia didn't stop. Sharon grabbed hold of my sleeve.

'Merlin went over,' she hiccuped.

'I know.'

'On his own!'

'Nia! Merlin's on his own,' we whispered one across the other.

But Nia couldn't stop. No more could the rest of us. One leap took her over the fence into the snapping crackling woods. We leapt after her, forged our way across to the Ribbon and scrambled hand over hand up its banks, kicking and bumping against each other, not even stopping to take a breath till we got to the flat rock.

'We'd better spread out,' gasped Nia, 'in case it's too late already. We'll all work our way separately up to the nest, covering as much ground as we can. That way one of us should find Edmund. He's not going to get away with it.'

She let herself slip down the bank straight into the water. The spray stung like ice. We helped each other up the bank and fanned out. Nia and Sharon ran straight across into the woods, Daniel headed upstream and I moved diagonally towards the nest. Twigs crackled beneath cautious feet and then all of a sudden the others were gone, leaving the woods full of my breathing. Behind me the sun sat balanced on top of the hill, sending fiery red shadows springing through the trees.

At first the shadows were silent, then, as I panted

up the slope, I heard crackling and rushing. I'd never really expected to see Edmund, but there he was running down towards me from out of the shadows. I thought it was a trick of the light and stood so still that when at last he saw me, the ground slid from under him and he came rolling, crashing, down at my feet.

'Gary!' he gasped.

'Get away!' I croaked. I could see his hands were empty, so I didn't have to feel angry about the eggs. I just didn't want him to touch me.

'Gar ...'

'Get away from Glaslyn!'

'Listen ...'

I looked down on him.

'You're a liar and a cheat!' I cried. 'The police are looking for you, Edmund Leggett.'

He flinched, then slid away from me and pulled himself up.

'They know who you are, so you'll never get away.' I followed him, wishing my words could hurt like hailstones.

'You leave the kite's nest alone.'

He stiffened and stared like Sid through the trees. His cheeks were too pink. There was light in his eyes and he wasn't even listening to me.

'You'll never get away.' I made a lunge for his arm. I wanted to hurt him for cheating me.

'Go home, Gary.'

'The police'll get you.'

'Go tell the police if you like. Tell them I'm up here. Go on!' He shook me away.

'I will too!' I wasn't joking. The others would be guarding the nest by now, so it was all right for me to go home. Let him try and stop me. As soon as I started running, twigs crackled behind me. I felt his breath on my shoulder, but when I swung round with my chest bursting, he wasn't there, just a smell clinging. The Ribbon came rushing across my path and I let myself slide, then struggled up towards the dark ranks of pine trees that smelled like Dad's wellies when he leaves them too close to the fire.

It was dark. I ran down in between the trees with my arms flung out. A glow-worm of light danced before me, then another, till suddenly smoke flooded down stinging like needles and sparks whirled like mosquitoes round my head.

'Gary!'

Someone was calling, but I couldn't answer. I couldn't open my mouth because it burned. The trees kept on getting in my way. My cheeks were smarting where the smoke had licked them dry. I clutched at a tree only for it to slide away from me.

'Gary!'

A dark shape was staggering towards me. I fell at its feet and it dragged me over the forest floor. I couldn't breathe. I couldn't stop the dragging. Pine needles wormed through my jeans and then I was rolling like a barrel. A wave of ice-cold water hit my face.

'Gary! Go back down the stream. Go back down the stream. Can you hear me?' Edmund's grey face came swimming towards me. 'Come on!'

An arm hitched itself round me and dragged me down the bed of the Ribbon. I couldn't get away from it. A pine tree exploded and showered us with sparks.

Suddenly Edmund was gone. The Ribbon started churning and something like a tidal wave swept down behind me.

'Gar!' I heard Nia squeak with alarm behind my back. 'The wood's on fire!' She pulled at my arm and I fell back against her. We both sat down with a bump in the middle of the water. Her face bent over me. 'Are you okay?' she whispered. 'You look horrible, Gar. What happened? Why didn't you come to the nest?' She put her arm round me.

'I ... I walked into the fire,' I said, choking on the taste of the smoke on my breath. My head fell against her shoulder. 'I didn't know where I was going. Then Edmund came ...'

Nia gasped at the sound of his name. 'Where is he?' she cried. 'Has he gone back to the nest?' The smoke was closing like a lid above our heads, crossing the Ribbon from bank to bank. 'Gar!' She pushed my weight off her shoulder. 'He must have started the fire to stop us getting to the nest. We were there, Sharon and Daniel and I were, and the RSPB man, but the RSPB man sent us away when he saw the sparks.'

Nia was lurching to her feet and pulling me with her. A wave of smoke dipped down and sucked at our clothes.

'We've got to stop him, Gary,' she said in a thick voice. 'We've got to go back and help the RSPB man.'

She wanted me to follow her up into that horrible smoke. Already I could feel it scrape my face. It was all around us, drifting in long lazy fingers. Looking back as we crawled up the bank, we could see it gush through the pine trees into a red sky lit up with sparks.

'Poor woods!' choked Nia, as we stumbled through the beech trees. 'Poor woods.'

'Sssh,' I whispered thinly through my teeth. I was trying to hang on to the noise of the Ribbon. Like a rope it hung down the valley. Once we lost it, we were on our own. 'Ssssh!' I whispered louder to the trees. The trees were crackling, rustling as if a great wind were tearing at their roots. Even Nia hesitated. Then a man came rushing out of the darkness around us.

'Ed ...!' began Nia.

But the man who crossed our path was bigger and wearing a kagoule just like Jeff's. He plunged on down the slope without a sideways glance.

'The RSPB man!' whispered Nia in the silence that followed his retreating footsteps. 'Now he's gone too. Gar ...'

Nia's nails dug into my hand. I knew what she was

going to say. It was too dangerous to go on. Of course it was. But before we could turn and follow the RSPB man to safety, a frantic noise echoed down through the trees, a noise as of canvas flapping in a gale. The kites were overhead. Their shadows wheeled across the sky, their great wings batting smoke. The kites were calling us.

'Edmund's got to the nest!' groaned Nia. 'Oh, it isn't fair!'

We stumbled towards the shadows of the kites, then before we knew it, we began to run. Faster and faster we moved back up the slope, seeming to trample bushes, elbow trees aside. The night was closing over us when Nia, who was just ahead of me, ran straight into the dark shape of Jeff's tent. She fell floundering against its side and from the darkness at her feet another shape rose.

'Nia!' I screamed.

Nia threw herself round my neck. Something was scratching and clawing at the side of Jeff's tent. Nia jerked me back. A hand reached up from the darkness and tried to snatch at my arm.

'It's Edmund!' Nia squealed. 'It's Edmund. He must have fallen from the kite tree.'

The hand came for me again. It missed and Edmund fell face down in the grass.

'Edmund?' I edged forward with Nia hanging on and tried to touch him. He struggled round and gripped so hard he nearly pulled me down. 'Don't!' I cried. He made a horrible wheezing noise and heaved himself up on his knees. He tried to get hold of Nia on his other side but she wouldn't let him. She dodged just out of reach.

'Edmund,' she said in a pinched voice. 'Where are the eggs?'

'Gone ...'

Nia lifted her face like a howling dog. Above our heads the kites spiralled away casting desperate shadows against the greying sky.

'Why?' wailed Nia. She was too despairing even to be angry. 'Those eggs belonged to the kite and the kite belongs to us all. Now everything's ruined for everybody.'

A glowing twig came floating down from the sky and briefly lit our faces. I didn't want any light. I didn't want to see the kite's eggs smashed to the ground where Edmund must have dropped them.

Nia and I reached down and without a word draped Edmund's arms around our shoulders. Angry fiery clouds raced above our heads and smoke gushed through the trees like dragon's breath chasing us down the hill. Edmund could have been a scarecrow for all I cared. I just wanted to get him out of the woods, then get rid of him. First we dragged him, then his legs started working and, as the ground began to slide beneath our feet and we zigzagged round the trees, he became lighter and lighter. We ran away from the smoke towards the fresh damp air that rose from the valley. On the air came strange noises and lights sparkled through the leaves.

As soon as we got clear of the woods we saw that Glaslyn's roads were ablaze. Ribbons of light wove their way round the village. Our kitchen door was open and Mam was standing framed in its light, quite still, with her head turned towards the flames that leapt from the trees just beyond the forestry clearing.

'Mam!'

It wasn't the sort of night when you could be heard in Glaslyn. I let go of Edmund, who pushed me over the fence. I began to run across the field heavy-legged over tussocks and potholes. Something came hurtling like a cannonball across the grass and threw itself against me. The something leapt away and ran purring back towards the house.

'Gary!' Daniel's voice came quavering to meet me. I could see him standing etched on top of the hedge and never seeming to get any nearer. 'Nia!'

'Gary! Nia!' The yell was picked up. A shadow left our doorstep, filled out and became Mam. Sid nearly got squashed between us, when we collided on the field side of the fence.

'Gary!' Mam gasped. The blue light of a police car slid across her face. 'Oh, someone had better tell your father quick. He's up in the woods. So's Nia's mam.'

Nia had flopped on the grass with Sharon and Daniel in attendance.

'The kite's eggs have gone!' she wailed. 'Edmund ruined them.'

Our lane was full of people heading up to the woods. The light of a police car pulsated across the empty fields and the fire sent flickering shadows along the valley. Pine trees exploded, died, exploded again.

'Is Dad okay, Mam?' I whispered.

'Lots of people went to try and beat out the fire before the fire engines arrived,' said Mam, sliding her arm round me. 'Your dad went with them. He'll be back.'

'Edmund rescued me from the fire, Mam.' I dragged my eyes away from the woods and risked a peep at her face. Her cheeks were pink in the firelight.

'Edmund?'

'He was after the kite's eggs.'

'Where is he?' Her grip tightened.

'He set fire to the woods ...'

'Where is he?' she demanded.

'It's all right. We got him out.'

Mam had let go of me. She had climbed up the hedge and was leaning, swaying on the sagging wire and searching amid the smoky shadows for Edmund. But Edmund had gone. We were quits. He'd saved me from the fire and Nia and I'd got him down from the woods. It was up to him now to get away from Glaslyn, if he could. Already Nia was running down the road looking for a policeman.

Smoke drifted in and out of our house. The yard was

108

full of jostling shadows and pale shapes. Dad pushed his way through them, blackened with ash.

'Gary!' He nearly smothered me. Sid's ears wouldn't stop twitching with excitement. 'Are you all right?'

'Yes!'

Dad smelled of smoke and pine trees and rubber.

'Someone started a fire with tyres in the woods,' he said savagely. 'It could have killed you. There's some old van up in the woods.'

'It's a forestry van.'

'Not a forestry van. It's meant to look like it, though. Someone's painted a yellow stripe on a green van. The police think that someone was after the kite's nest.'

'It was Ed ...' I stopped. Mam was coming towards us.

'Edmund saved Gary from the fire,' she said crisply. 'He came out of the woods with Gary, but we don't know where he is.'

I squeezed Dad's arm.

'We've got to find him,' she said. 'I can't think why he's disappeared.'

'Mam!' It had to be the Perrott business again. Why couldn't she understand? He had tried to steal the kite eggs. He'd set fire to the woods. That was reason enough for disappearing.

'What do you know about the van anyway?' Dad asked sharply.

'Nothing. It was just ...' I could smell it again, the

smell of turps that had followed us from the quarry to the woods via One Night Cottage.

'Gary,' said Mam in a low voice. She could tell by my face that something had clicked. 'What is it?'

Dad raised his eyebrows. I turned away to try to sort out things in my mind, the smell of turps, the painted van.

'There was paint, yellow paint, in One Night Cottage,' I blurted out.

'One Night Cottage!' echoed Mam.

Before Dad and I could stop her, she'd gone running to the fence as though a button had been pressed inside her. Dad's breath exploded out of him. Nan and Dad-cu Lloyd were coming down the road and were calling to us. We heard their voices, but we couldn't stop. We had to follow Mam.

'Dilys,' yelled Dad.

Mam was drifting across the lumpy field in front of us like one of those women in folk tales whose feet are buried in mist. Billowy mounds of sheep huddled scared against the hedges with their green eyes blinking away the smoke.

The valley had changed into a smoggy city with hundreds of burning lights. Our footsteps echoed on the damp grass and our breath made patterns in the smoke. As soon as we went over the hillock behind Nia's house, One Night Cottage rose up out of its own private island of mist with flame-shadows sweeping its walls.

'Dad!' I said. 'There's a man staying in the cottage.

It won't be just Edmund. It could be dangerous.'

'Dil!' hissed Dad through his teeth, but Mam was already coming to a halt beside the straggly sheep-munched hedge that separates the cottage from the field. A click had echoed in the cottage garden and, as we reached Mam, a car engine burst into life. We pulled Mam back from the dark shape that bucked and crashed into trees and bushes. The headlights flashed on and the shadow of a man ran through the beam to the driver's door.

'Get out of my car!' he roared.

Dad plunged straight through the straggly hedge.

'Edmund!' he called. 'Are you there, Edmund?'

The man swung round and lunged at Dad with his fists. It was the RSPB man who'd passed Nia and myself in the woods. Mam screamed. At that moment the car stopped jerking. Its horn blared and went on blaring over Glaslyn.

Edmund jumped out. Something jingled through the air and landed with a distant thud in the sheep field. The man beside the car froze with his fists up and just as suddenly he melted. His hands dropped by his sides and swiftly he merged with the darkness at the back of the cottage.

Edmund opened the car door, snatched something from inside and made a dash past Dad towards the lane.

'Let him go!' cried Mam in a brittle voice. 'Howell, let him go!'

'Come on!' Dad came running back to us. He

caught hold of Mam's arm and bundled us both through the hedge, through the garden and out into the lane. We were running up towards the road when we saw the blue light of a police car stop at the junction ahead of us. We heard Edmund's voice, high-pitched, echo through the night. Then the door slammed and the car accelerated away.

A shower of sparks flew over our heads and by their light I saw that Mam was smiling.

'Why are you smiling?' I asked with a shiver.

'Because you and Dad and I are still together,' she said. 'That's all that matters.'

She linked arms and the three of us turned for home.

Nia, Daniel and Sharon were crouching on the mat in front of our Rayburn.

'They've got Edmund,' I said, crouching beside them. 'The police have got him.'

'But it's too late,' snuffled Nia with her face buried in her arms. 'We've failed. We can't call ourselves the Kite Gang any more.'

Mam was standing in the doorway. When I looked round, the smoke made her seem taller and she had a calmness about her that I hadn't seen since the E. M. Perrott affair began.

'I wonder,' she said.

'Why?' I crept towards her across the floor and huddled at her feet. We looked down at a winking blue light that was following another car down Nia's farm lane.

'Why's that police car going to Nia's house?' I asked.

'Perhaps you should go down and see.' Mam smiled.

We all four left together. All along the road there were people clustered at the fence like swallows ready to fly. Shouts echoed from the burning woods. Though the fire was dying down, it had eaten a dark hole in the hillside. I was glad to turn down into the shelter of Nia's lane, where all we could see was the light of Nia's kitchen beaming out across the yard. Shadows began moving across this light as we crept like shadows ourselves towards the open door.

It was daft, but at that moment I began to feel scared again. The shadows were like waves ebbing and flowing towards us. Even Nia seemed scared of crossing her own doorstep.

Then, 'Jeff!' she breathed.

The rest of us crowded behind her.

Jeff Jones and another man we'd never seen before were standing at Nia's kitchen table beside a large plastic container with a light inside. Into the container they were putting straw that Nia's mam had just warmed in the Rayburn.

Not one of us moved ... or spoke.

We couldn't believe what was going to happen next. Jeff reached for a hard leather binoculars' case that was standing on the table. From a thick bed of cotton wool inside he took out two white splodgy eggs.

'The kite's eggs!' Nia gasped. 'They're all right!'

Jeff put them inside the plastic box and closed the door. We were too afraid to breathe. It was Jeff who spoke.

'There,' he said. 'With luck we could still have kite chicks, thanks to you.'

For a moment I thought he meant thanks to us, but that couldn't be right. He wasn't even looking at us. He was speaking to someone in the corner of the room. The four of us edged round the door and bumped into each other in shock. Edmund was sitting on the settee by the Rayburn, his face china white with a pink weal on his forehead.

Jeff's companion drew his sleeve over his face. He looked across at us and whispered in a husky voice, 'I left the nest as soon as I first smelled the fire. I went to get help. I thought that was best, but if it hadn't been for ...'

'For Edmund?' I said incredulously.

'If it hadn't been for Edmund we'd have lost the eggs,' beamed Jeff. He flung out his arms as if he wanted to hug us all. 'Edmund chased the egg collector to One Night Cottage and got the eggs back for us.'

'But ...' Nia's mouth looked as if a hinge had come loose. She couldn't close it. Lucky it was too early in the year for gnats or she'd have trapped enough to feed a swallow for a month.

'That man we saw in the woods,' I said to her. 'He

was the man in One Night Cottage. You said he was the RSPB man.'

'Well, that's what he said,' said Nia with a scowl. 'That's what he said.'

'Well, he wasn't,' said Jeff. 'The other RSPB man is my friend Dylan here.'

Dylan and Jeff's faces were shiny bright in the light from the incubator. The rest of us were trying to get things straight. If Edmund hadn't gone up the tree to get the kite's eggs, why had he been hiding in the woods? We just couldn't take our eyes off him, all four of us. It was as if they were glued. In the end, in self-defence, Edmund grinned. And then we all started grinning. After all, what can you do but grin when there are two live kite eggs sitting in front of you in an incubator? There'd be time for explanations later.

'Are we going to hatch them here?' Nia asked, moving respectfully towards the eggs on tiptoe.

'No,' smiled Jeff. 'We'll have to take them away for safekeeping, as soon as we're sure they're okay.'

'Oh!' sighed Nia.

But she couldn't grumble. It's a rare privilege to have a living kite egg in your home even for one minute. Jeff stayed for nearly an hour, before driving the incubator away under police escort.

Then it was Edmund's turn to be rushed to hospital for a check-up but first we made him tell us how he'd

saved the kite eggs.

It's funny. After all the watching the Kite Gang
did, we missed the most obvious thing – the forestry
van. Two forestry vans, in fact. Jeff was using a real
one. The other wasn't a forestry van at all, but just an
ordinary dark green van with a painted yellow stripe
that the egg collector had been using to get to the
forest and search for the nest. Edmund had to tell us
all about it.

'I found an empty yellow paint tin in the quarry,'
he explained. 'And some turps.'

'Turps,' echoed Sharon.

'And I was really mad because the turps had
spilled over some dead bird that was in the quarry. I
thought it was a danger to the kites if they ate it.'

'Was that why you threw something at Merlin to
make him go away?' asked Nia humbly.

116

'Yes.'

Nia nodded.

'Then I remembered the paint on the gatepost at the cottage.'

'That's right.' I remembered it too.

'And I wondered why a holidaymaker would need yellow paint, so I went to have a look at the cottage. Just as I was getting there a van pulled out. Now I'd heard a van or something rumble past Gary's house in the night, very quietly and without any lights, so . . .'

'Huh!' said Nia. 'And Gary didn't hear a thing, I suppose.'

'Well . . .' I would have rounded on her, but she was grinning for once. What else can you do but grin, as I said before, when you've just had live kite eggs in your house?

'So last night I went up to the woods, found the van and tried to keep watch on it from the den. But the guy had disappeared. Then today when he started the fire, he took me by surprise and I didn't know whether to put out the fire or follow him to the ne . . . st.' Edmund suddenly realised everyone was looking at him and nearly choked on his tonsils.

'Then . . . Then I found Gary and by the time I got to the nest, the man was coming down the tree,' he said hastily. 'He kicked me to the ground and I hit my head. That's when you found me.'

Nia went on staring at his pink face.

'And to think that we thought you were a crook!'

117

she said at last, hitting her head hard with the flat of her hand. 'Honestly! How daft can you get?'

Edmund laughed. The other three crowded round him like the best of friends. They'd all forgotten he was still in our valley under false pretences.

Our valley smelled of burning. The fire had died, but the lights of the fire engines sparkled through the stark pine trees and a hum of voices and machinery drifted over the fields.

Mam and Dad were in the yard saying goodbye to Nan and Dad-cu Lloyd. Smoke came oozing thinly from our kitchen door.

'Where's Edmund?' whispered Mam, coming back into the house with her hands tucked into her sleeves.

'He's gone for a check-up,' I said. 'He saved the kite eggs.'

I watched her.

'You were right, you know,' I said at last.

'What about?' She was looking very calm and peaceful like the Mam I used to know.

'Well, he never was an egg thief,' I said. 'So he must be a Perrott.'

'Oh no!' Mam laughed at herself. 'That was me being stupid. He's not a Perrott at all. He ... but then of course you don't know, because you were up in the woods when we found out. The police told us. They'd been asked to watch out for an Edmund Leggett, who'd left home after a disagreement with his parents. They thought he might be heading this way.'

'Why?' I watched the smoke slowly melt and the sheep start moving again in the fields. I knew the answer already.

'Because of the kites,' said Mam. 'He's keen on birds and wants to be an ornithologist, but his dad, who's a solicitor in Preston – not London – was putting pressure on him to study law and join the family firm. They'd been quarrelling a lot about it.'

'That's daft,' I said.

I meant it was daft not letting Edmund do what he wanted, but Mam took it another way.

'Yes,' she said, slipping her arm into mine. 'It's daft to quarrel. Who needs Perrotts anyway? When I think that that egg thief not only nearly killed two kite chicks, but he nearly killed you as well. Those two poor kites flapping away in the sky could have been Dad and I.'

April 21st

Nia rang.

'No sign of the kites,' she said gloomily.

The pine trees in Glaslyn are blacker than trees in winter, like strange black fingers pointing to the sky. The beeches and oaks were saved by the Ribbon. But who wants to live in a semi when the house next

119

door has burnt down? I expect that's how the kites feel.

'Look at what the egg thief has done,' I told Mam. 'Just because he wanted eggs so much, he's ruined Glaslyn.'

'Yes.' Mam was cooking, attacking the pastry like mad and sending up floury smoke signals. She shook back the hair from her eyes. 'Yes,' she said. 'You can't just go after what you want and not think about anyone else.'

She attacked the pastry again. More clouds of flour rose up in distress and melted all over the kitchen.

It had gone by the time Edmund and his mam and dad arrived, but only just. Edmund's parents had driven down from Preston to pick him up at the hospital and had brought him back to our place. They arrived unexpectedly early.

Mam gave a desperate squawk and rushed upstairs to get out of her cooking clothes, while I threw dirty dishes into the sink. Luckily Sid Radish is good at delaying tactics.

This is how Sid does it:
1. He parks himself on the path in front of the unsuspecting visitors.
2. He stares.
3. When the visitors have been mesmerised by his stare, Sid allows himself to be spoken to.
4. When the visitors are cooing: 'Hello, pussy-cat,'

Sid gets up, stretches his large sleek form and stalks over to show he's not your ordinary pussy-cat, but a proud close relation of the Kings of the Jungle.

5. He walks round the visitors once, then pads nobly into the house with his tail in the air.

While all this was going on, I was madly clearing up, Mam was flinging on a clean dress, Dad was shooting out of the front room where he'd just laid a fire, with a dustpan in his hand. Thanks to Sid, we all got to the door on time.

Edmund Leggett.

As he stood there with his mam and dad on either side of him, I saw him properly for the very first time. He was just an ordinary boy, seventeen, a bit thin and pale, but friendly-looking.

Mam and Dad swept Mr and Mrs Leggett into the house.

'Are you okay?' I asked, slipping out of the door to stand beside him.

'Yes.' He was looking across the valley. 'But the kites have gone,' he said sadly.

'They'll come back. Jeff said so. You can come down here and see them. They'll be around to breed again next year,' I said more firmly than I felt.

Edmund raised his eyebrows. He sat down on the wall in front of the kitchen window.

'They will,' I said to try and nudge the frown away from his face.

'I suppose so,' he sighed. 'It's just that there are so

few of them and so many people out to get them and so many things that could harm them. That quarry's full of old muck that could kill kites.'

'We'll clear it,' I said. 'And we'll put up notices to stop people dumping things. It'll give the Kite Gang something to do. We'll do it before the chicks come.'

'What chicks?' Mr Leggett had come out behind us.

'The kite chicks,' I said, only Edmund could explain better than I could. As he explained, his father watched him and I think his father was more excited by the look on Edmund's face than by the story of the chicks.

Edmund is mad about kites, which is lucky for us. That's how he came to Glaslyn and saved the eggs.

He's as mad as Jeff Jones.

As mad as any of us.

Which is amazing, considering he doesn't even come from our village.

Mam doesn't come from Glaslyn either. Later I showed Edmund the tree map I'd drawn with Dad and me at the bottom and Mam on a branch.

I drew a nest on the tree and another long spindly branch with 'To Preston' on it. It was Edmund's branch and Edmund was pleased to be part of the kite's tree, till I went on to tell him about the Perrott and how Mam had got him mixed up. I saw him look sheepishly at Mam when she called us in to have

← To preston

← To manchester

Kite Country

The tree map again!

tea together before Edmund and his family went home.

April 29th: The quarry's been cleaned up.
April 30th: We're waiting.
May 1st: Ten
May 2nd: Nine
May 3rd: Eight
May 4th: Seven
May 5th: Six
May 6th: Five
May 7th: The eggs hatched out!
We didn't have time to finish our countdown.
The eggs hatched out!
Two new kites in Glaslyn. (Well, they're not in Glaslyn yet, but they soon will be.)
This is the most secret hatching ever! Only the RSPB, the Kite Gang and a few others know about it.
And you!
Don't tell!
I've seen them. They're pink and scrawny and unkite-like.
We had a massive late Easter egg in our HQ to celebrate. Now all that's left is for the chicks to fly.

June 28th: KNOCK ME DOWN (with a kite feather)!

124

Edmund's dad phoned up. He's traced Eileen Mary Brown (née Perrott) to an address in Yorkshire. He did it to thank us, so he said, and Edmund helped him. I suppose they're nearer to Manchester than we are and they're used to things like that, being solicitors.

Dad was stunned.

Mam is ... scared.

Merlin the Kite is flying over the quarry and new trees are being planted in the burnt patch on the slope.

Mam is leaving tomorrow for Yorkshire.

Dad and I are being left alone.

(Sorry, Sid is here too. He reminded me by flicking the notebook off my lap with his paw and giving me the Sid stare.)

July 30th

Stare.

That's all you can do when your long-lost gran is coming up the yard.

She's got Mam's and my hair. Only she's short and stumpy and shifty like Edmund was when he was trying to be a Kipling. And she speaks with a strange accent.

'Mam?'

Mam knows her already – and she's met her new

125

half-sister up in Yorkshire.

'Show your gran into the house, there's a good boy. This is Gary.'

Nan and Dad-cu Rees are here as well and Sid is fed up with squeezing against our legs and no one taking any notice of him. Sid is so fed up, he gives a bloodcurdling screech and bolts out dramatically through the kitchen door.

'What's wrong, Sid?'

It's my excuse to bolt out after him.

'Si-iiiiid! Si ... !'

Then I see it.

There's a kite over the quarry.

A small kite!

Everybody comes out – Nan and Dad-cu Rees, Gran Brown and her husband, Dad, Mam. Only Gran and Mr Brown don't know what it is, that shape in the sky.

'That's a very special chick,' I tell them. 'A chick that we brought up.'

Gran Brown looks at Nan Rees and we all of us laugh.

Gran thinks I mean Mam.

My Mother-Kite.

Join the RED FOX Reader's Club

The Red Fox Reader's Club is for readers of all ages. All you have to do is ask your local bookseller or librarian for a Red Fox Reader's Club card. As an official Red Fox Reader you only have to borrow or buy eight Red Fox books in order to qualify for your own Red Fox Reader's Clubpack – full of exciting surprises! If you have any difficulty obtaining a Red Fox Reader's Club card please write to: Random House Children's Books Marketing Department, 20 Vauxhall Bridge Road, London SW1V 2SA.